Edward Bulwer

The Parisians

Edward Bulwer

The Parisians

ISBN/EAN: 9783742821836

Manufactured in Europe, USA, Canada, Australia, Japa

Cover: Foto ©Andreas Hilbeck / pixelio.de

Manufactured and distributed by brebook publishing software
(www.brebook.com)

Edward Bulwer

The Parisians

COLLECTION

OF

BRITISH AUTHORS

TAUCHNITZ EDITION.

VOL. 1359.

THE PARISIANS

BY

EDWARD BULWER, LORD LYTTON.

IN FOUR VOLUMES. — VOL. I.

LEIPZIG: BERNHARD TAUCHNITZ

PARIS: C. REINWALD & Cⁱᵉ, 15, RUE DES SAINTS PÈRES.

COLLECTION

OF

BRITISH AUTHORS

TAUCHNITZ EDITION.

VOL. 1359.

THE PARISIANS BY E. BULWER, LORD LYTTON.

IN FOUR VOLUMES.

VOL. I.

TAUCHNITZ EDITION.

By the same Author,

THE PARISIANS

BY

EDWARD BULWER, LORD LYTTON,

AUTHOR OF

'PELHAM,' 'KENELM CHILLINGLY.'

COPYRIGHT EDITION.

IN FOUR VOLUMES.—VOL. I.

LEIPZIG

BERNHARD TAUCHNITZ

1873.

INTRODUCTORY CHAPTER.

THEY who chance to have read the 'Coming Race' may perhaps remember that I, the adventurous discoverer of the land without a sun, concluded the sketch of my adventures by a brief reference to the malady which, though giving no perceptible notice of its encroachments, might, in the opinion of my medical attendant, prove suddenly fatal.

I had brought my little book to this somewhat melancholy close a few years before the date of its publication, and, in the meanwhile, I was induced to transfer my residence to Paris, in order to place myself under the care of an English physician, renowned for his successful treatment of complaints analogous to my own.

I was the more readily persuaded to undertake this journey, partly because I enjoyed a familiar acquaintance with the eminent physician referred to, who had

commenced his career and founded his reputation in
the United States, partly because I had become a
solitary man, the ties of home broken, and dear friends
of mine were domiciled in Paris, with whom I should
be sure of tender sympathy and cheerful companionship.
I had reason to be thankful for this change of residence: the skill of Dr C—— soon restored me to
health. Brought much into contact with various circles of Parisian society, I became acquainted with the
persons, and a witness of the events, that form the
substance of the tale I am about to submit to the
public, which has treated my former book with so
generous an indulgence. Sensitively tenacious of that
character for strict and unalloyed veracity, which, I
flatter myself, my account of the abodes and manners
of the Vril-ya has established, I could have wished to
preserve the following narrative no less jealously guarded
than its predecessor from the vagaries of fancy.
But Truth undisguised, never welcome in any civilised community above ground, is exposed at this
time to especial dangers in Paris; and my life would
not be worth an hour's purchase if I exhibited her
in puris naturalibus to the eyes of a people wholly
unfamiliarised to a spectacle so indecorous. That
care for one's personal safety, which is the first duty

of thoughtful man, compels me therefore to reconcile the appearance of *la Vérité* to the *bienséances* of the polished society in which *la Liberté* admits no opinion not dressed after the last fashion.

Attired as fiction, Truth may be peacefully received; and, despite the necessity thus imposed by prudence, I indulge the modest hope that I do not in these pages unfaithfully represent certain prominent types of the brilliant population which has invented so many varieties of Koom-Posh;* and even when it appears hopelessly lost in the slough of a Glek-Nas, re-emerges fresh and lively as if from an invigorating plunge into the Fountain of Youth. *O Paris, foyer des idées, et œil du monde!*—animated contrast to the serene tranquillity of the Vril-ya, which, nevertheless, thy noisiest philosophers ever pretend to make the goal of their desires—of all communities on which shines the sun and descend the rains of heaven, fertilising alike wisdom and folly, virtue and vice, in

---

* Koom-Posh, Glek-Nas. For the derivation of these terms and their metaphorical signification, I must refer the reader to the 'Coming Race,' chapter XII., on the language of the Vril-ya. To those who have not read or have forgotten that historical composition, it may be convenient to state briefly that Koom-Posh with the Vril-ya is the name for the government of the many, or the ascendancy of the most ignorant or hollow, and may be loosely rendered Hollow-Bosh. When Koom-Posh degenerates from popular ignorance into the popular ferocity which precedes its decease, the name for that state of things is Glek-Nas—viz., the universal strife-rot.

every city men have yet built on this earth, mayest thou, O Paris, be the last to brave the wands of the Coming Race and be reduced into cinders for the sake of the common good!

TISH.

PARIS, *August* 28, 1872.

BOOK I.

Google

THE PARISIANS.

BOOK I.

CHAPTER I.

IT was a bright day in the early spring of 1869. All Paris seemed to have turned out to enjoy itself. The Tuileries, the Champs Elysées, the Bois de Boulogne, swarmed with idlers. A stranger might have wondered where Toil was at work, and in what nook Poverty lurked concealed. A *millionnaire* from the London Exchange, as he looked round on the *magasins*, the equipages, the dresses of the women; as he inquired the prices in the shops and the rent of apartments,—might have asked himself, in envious wonder, How on earth do those gay Parisians live? What is their fortune? Where does it come from?

As the day declined, many of the scattered loungers crowded into the Boulevards; the *cafés* and *restaurants* began to light up.

About this time a young man, who might be some five or six and twenty, was walking along the Boulevard des Italiens, heeding little the throng through which he glided his solitary way: there was that in his aspect

and bearing which caught attention. He looked a
somebody; but though unmistakably a Frenchman, not
a Parisian. His dress was not in the prevailing mode,—
to a practised eye it betrayed the taste and the cut of
a provincial tailor. His gait was not that of the
Parisian—less lounging, more stately; and, unlike the
Parisian, he seemed indifferent to the gaze of others.

Nevertheless there was about him that air of dignity
or distinction which those who are reared from their
cradle in the pride of birth acquire so unconsciously
that it seems hereditary and inborn. It must also be
confessed that the young man himself was endowed
with a considerable share of that nobility which Nature capriciously distributes among her favourites, with
little respect for their pedigree and blazon—the nobility of form and face. He was tall and well shaped,
with graceful length of limb and fall of shoulders;
his face was handsome, of the purest type of French
masculine beauty—the nose inclined to be aquiline,
and delicately thin, with finely-cut open nostrils; the
complexion clear, the eyes large, of a light hazel, with
dark lashes, the hair of a chestnut brown, with no tint
of auburn, the beard and moustache a shade darker,
clipped short, not disguising the outline of lips, which
were now compressed, as if smiles had of late been
unfamiliar to them; yet such compression did not seem
in harmony with the physiognomical character of their
formation, which was that assigned by Lavater to
temperaments easily moved to gaiety and pleasure.

Another man, about his own age, coming quickly

out of one of the streets of the Chaussée d'Antin,
brushed close by the stately pedestrian above described,
caught sight of his countenance, stopped short, and
exclaimed, "Alain!" The person thus abruptly accosted
turned his eye tranquilly on the eager face, of which
all the lower part was enveloped in black beard; and
slightly lifting his hat, with a gesture of the head that
implied, "Sir, you are mistaken; I have not the honour
to know you," continued his slow indifferent way. The
would-be acquaintance was not so easily rebuffed.
"*Peste*," said he, between his teeth, "I am certainly
right. He is not much altered—of course *I am;* ten
years of Paris would improve an orang-outang." Quick-
ening his step, and regaining the side of the man he
had called "Alain," he said, with a well-bred mixture
of boldness and courtesy in his tone and countenance—

"Ten thousand pardons if I am wrong. But surely
I accost Alain de Kerouec, son of the Marquis de
Rochebriant."

"True, sir; but——"

"But you do not remember me, your old college
friend, Frederic Lemercier!"

"Is it possible!" cried Alain, cordially, and with
an animation which changed the whole character of
his countenance. "My dear Frederic, my dear friend,
this is indeed good fortune! So you, too, are at
Paris!"

"Of course; and you! Just come, I perceive," he
added, somewhat satirically, as, linking his arm in his

new-found friend's, he glanced at the cut of that friend's coat-collar.

"I have been here a fortnight," replied Alain.

"Hem! I suppose you lodge in the old Hotel de Rochebriant. I passed it yesterday, admiring its vast *façade*, little thinking you were its inmate."

"Neither am I; the hotel does not belong to me —it was sold some years ago by my father."

"Indeed! I hope your father got a good price for it; those grand hotels have trebled their value within the last five years. And how is your father? Still the same polished *grand seigneur?* I never saw him but once, you know: and I shall never forget his smile, *style grand monarque*, when he patted me on the head and tipped me ten napoleons."

"My father is no more," said Alain, gravely; "he has been dead nearly three years."

"*Ciel!* forgive me, I am greatly shocked. Hem! so you are now the Marquis de Rochebriant, a great historical name, worth a large sum in the market. Few such names left. Superb place your old chateau, is it not?"

"A superb place, No—a venerable ruin, Yes!"

"Ah, a ruin! so much the better. All the bankers are mad after ruins —so charming an amusement to restore them. You will restore yours, without doubt. I will introduce you to such an architect! has the *moyen âge* at his fingers' ends. Dear—but a genius."

The young Marquis smiled—for since he had

found a college friend, his face showed that it could smile; smiled, but not cheerfully, and answered—

"I have no intention to restore Rochebriant. The walls are solid; they have weathered the storms of six centuries; they will last my time, and with me the race perishes."

"Bah! the race perish, indeed! you will marry. *Parlez-moi de ça*—you could not come to a better man. I have a list of all the heiresses at Paris, bound in russia leather. You may take your choice out of twenty. Ah, if I were but a Rochebriant! It is an infernal thing to come into the world a Lemercier. I am a democrat, of course. A Lemercier would be in a false position if he were not. But if any one would leave me twenty acres of land, with some antique right to the De and a title, faith, would not I be an aristocrat, and stand up for my order? But now we have met, pray let us dine together. Ah! no doubt you are engaged every day for a month. A Rochebriant just new to Paris must be *fêté* by all the Faubourg."

"No," answered Alain, simply—"I am not engaged; my range of acquaintance is more circumscribed than you suppose."

"So much the better for me. I am luckily disengaged to-day, which is not often the case, for I am in some request in my own set, though it is not that of the Faubourg. Where shall we dine?—at the Trois Frères?"

"Wherever you please. I know no *restaurant* at Paris except a very ignoble one, close by my lodging."

"*A propos*, where do you lodge?"

"Rue de l'Université, Numero * * * "

"A fine street, but *triste*. If you have no longer your family hotel, you have no excuse to linger in that museum of mummies, the Faubourg St. Germain; you must go into one of the new quarters by the Champs Elysées. Leave it to me; I'll find you a charming apartment. I know one to be had a bargain —a bagatelle—500 naps a-year. Cost you about two or three thousand more to furnish tolerably, not showily. Leave all to me. In three days you shall be settled. *A propos!* horses! You must have English ones. How many?—three for the saddle, two for your *coupé?* I'll find them for you. I will write to London to-morrow. *Reese* (Rice) is your man."

"Spare yourself that trouble, my dear Frederic. I keep no horses and no *coupé*. I shall not change my apartment." As he said this, Rochebriant drew himself up somewhat haughtily.

"Faith," thought Lemercier, "is it possible that the Marquis is poor? No. I have always heard that the Rochebriants were among the greatest proprietors in Bretagne. Most likely, with all his innocence of the Faubourg St. Germain, he knows enough of it to be aware that I, Frederic Lemercier, am not the man to patronise one of its greatest nobles. *Sacre bleu!* if I thought that; if he meant to give himself airs to me, his old college friend—I would—I would call him out."

Just as M. Lemercier had come to that bellicose resolution, the Marquis said, with a smile which, though frank, was not without a certain grave melancholy in its expression, "My dear Frederic, pardon me if I seem to receive your friendly offers ungraciously. But believe that I have reasons you will approve for leading at Paris a life which you certainly will not envy;" then, evidently desirous to change the subject, he said in a livelier tone, "But what a marvellous city this Paris of ours is! Remember I had never seen it before: it burst on me like a city in the Arabian Nights two weeks ago. And that which strikes me most—I say it with regret and a pang of conscience—is certainly not the Paris of former times, but that Paris which M. Buonaparte—I beg pardon, which the Emperor—has called up around him, and identified for ever with his reign. It is what is new in Paris that strikes and enthrals me. Here I see the life of France, and I belong to her tombs!"

"I don't quite understand you," said Lemercier. "If you think that because your father and grandfather were Legitimists, you have not the fair field of living ambition open to you under the Empire, you never were more mistaken. *Moyen âge*, and even *rococo*, are all the rage. You have no idea how valuable your name would be either at the Imperial Court or in a Commercial Company. But with your fortune you are independent of all but fashion and the Jockey

Club. And à propos of that, pardon me—what villain made your coat?—let me know; I will denounce him to the police."

Half amused, half amazed, Alain Marquis de Rochebriant looked at Frederic Lemercier much as a good-tempered lion may look upon a lively poodle who takes a liberty with his mane, and, after a pause, he replied curtly, "The clothes I wear at Paris were made in Bretagne; and if the name of Rochebriant be of any value at all in Paris, which I doubt, let me trust that it will make me acknowledged as *gentil-homme*, whatever my taste in a coat or whatever the doctrines of a club composed—of jockeys."

"Ha, ha!" cried Lemercier, freeing himself from the arm of his friend, and laughing the more irre-sistibly as he encountered the grave look of the Mar-quis. "Pardon me—I can't help it—the Jockey Club —composed of jockeys!—it is too much!—the best joke. My dear Alain, there is some of the best blood of Europe in the Jockey Club; they would exclude a plain *bourgeois* like me. But it is all the same; in one respect you are quite right. Walk in a *blouse* if you please—you are still Rochebriant—you would only be called eccentric. Alas! I am obliged to send to Lon-don for my pantaloons; that comes of being a Lemer-cier. But here we are in the Palais Royal."

CHAPTER IL

THE *salons* of the Trois Frères were crowded—
our friends found a table with some little difficulty.
Lemercier proposed a private cabinet, which, for some
reason known to himself, the Marquis declined.

Lemercier spontaneously and unrequested ordered
the dinner and the wines.

While waiting for their oysters, with which, when
in season, French *bon-vivants* usually commence their
dinner, Lemercier looked round the *salon* with that
air of inimitable, scrutinising, superb impertinence
which distinguishes the Parisian dandy. Some of the
ladies returned his glance coquettishly, for Lemercier
was *beau garçon;* others turned aside indignantly, and
muttered something to the gentlemen dining with
them. The said gentlemen, when old, shook their
heads, and continued to eat unmoved; when young,
turned briskly round, and looked at first fiercely at
M. Lemercier, but, encountering his eye through the
glass which he had screwed into its socket—noticing
the hardihood of his countenance and the squareness
of his shoulders—even they turned back to the tables,
shook their heads, and continued to eat unmoved, just
like the old ones.

"Ah!" cried Lemercier, suddenly, "here comes a

2*

man you should know, *mon cher.* He will tell you
how to place your money—a rising man—a coming
man—a future minister. Ah! *bon jour*, Duplessis, *bon
jour*," kissing his hand to a gentleman who had just
entered, and was looking about him for a seat. He
was evidently well and favourably known at the Trois
Frères. The waiters had flocked round him, and were
pointing to a table by the window, which a saturnine
Englishman, who had dined off a beefsteak and pota-
toes, was about to vacate.

Mons. Duplessis, having first assured himself, like
a prudent man, that his table was secure, having
ordered his oysters, his chablis, and his *potage à la
bisque*, now paced calmly and slowly across the *salon*,
and halted before Lemercier.

Here let me pause for a moment, and give the
reader a rapid sketch of the two Parisians.

Frederic Lemercier is dressed, somewhat too
showily, in the extreme of the prevalent fashion. He
wears a superb pin in his cravat—a pin worth 2000
francs; he wears rings on his fingers, *breloques* to his
watch-chain. He has a warm though dark complexion, thick black eyebrows, full lips, a nose somewhat turned up, but not small, very fine large dark
eyes, a bold, open, somewhat impertinent expression
of countenance—withal decidedly handsome, thanks
to colouring, youth, and vivacity of '*regard.*'

Lucien Duplessis, bending over the table, glancing
first with curiosity at the Marquis de Rochebriant, who
leans his cheek on his hand and seems not to notice

him, then concentrating his attention on Frederic
Lemercier, who sits square with his hands clasped—
Lucien Duplessis is somewhere between forty and
fifty, rather below the middle height, slender but not
slight—what in English phrase is called 'wiry'. He is
dressed with extreme simplicity: black frock-coat
buttoned up; black cravat worn higher than men who
follow the fashions wear their neckcloths nowadays; a
hawk's eye and a hawk's beak; hair of a dull brown,
very short, and wholly without curl; his cheeks thin
and smoothly shaven, but he wears a moustache and
imperial, plagiarised from those of his sovereign, and,
like all plagiarisms, carrying the borrowed beauty to
extremes, so that the points of moustache and imperial, stiffened and sharpened by cosmetics which
must have been composed of iron, looked like three
long stings guarding lip and jaw from invasion; a
pale olive-brown complexion; eyes small, deep-sunk,
calm, piercing; his expression of face at first glance
not striking, except for quiet immovability. Observed
more heedfully, the expression was keenly intellectual
—determined about the lips, calculating about the
brows: altogether the face of no ordinary man, and
one not, perhaps, without fine and high qualities, concealed from the general gaze by habitual reserve, but
justifying the confidence of those whom he admitted
into his intimacy.

"Ah, *mon cher*," said Lemercier, "you promised to
call on me yesterday at two o'clock. I waited in for
you half an hour; you never came."

"No; I went first to the *Bourse*. The shares in that Company we spoke of have fallen; they will fall much lower—foolish to buy in yet; so the object of my calling on you was over. I took it for granted you would not wait if I failed my appointment. Do you go to the opera to-night?"

"I think not—nothing worth going for; besides, I have found an old friend, to whom I consecrate this evening. Let me introduce you to the Marquis de Rochebriant. Alain, M. Duplessis."

The two gentlemen bowed.

"I had the honour to be known to Monsieur your father," said Duplessis.

"Indeed," returned Rochebriant. "He had not visited Paris for many years before he died."

"It was in London I met him, at the house of the Russian Princess C——."

The Marquis coloured high, inclined his head gravely, and made no reply. Here the waiter brought the oysters and the chablis, and Duplessis retired to his own table.

"That is the most extraordinary man," said Frederic, as he squeezed the lemon over his oysters, "and very much to be admired."

"How so! I see nothing at least to admire in his face," said the Marquis, with the bluntness of a provincial.

"His face. Ah! you are a Legitimist—party prejudice. He dresses his face after the Emperor; in itself a very clever face, surely."

"Perhaps, but not an amiable one. He looks like a bird of prey."

"All clever men are birds of prey. The eagles are the heroes, and the owls the sages. Duplessis is not an eagle nor an owl. I should rather call him a falcon, except that I would not attempt to hoodwink him."

"Call him what you will," said the Marquis, indifferently; "M. Duplessis can be nothing to me."

"I'm not so sure of that," answered Frederic, somewhat nettled by the phlegm with which the Provincial regarded the pretensions of the Parisian. "Duplessis, I repeat it, is an extraordinary man. Though untitled, he descends from your old aristocracy; in fact, I believe, as his name shows, from the same stem as the Richelieus. His father was a great scholar, and I believe he has read much himself. Might have distinguished himself in literature or at the bar, but his parents died fearfully poor; and some distant relations in commerce took charge of him, and devoted his talents to the *Bourse*. Seven years ago he lived in a single chamber, *au quatrième*, near the Luxembourg. He has now a hotel, not large but charming, in the Champs Elysées, worth at least 600,000 francs. Nor has he made his own fortune alone, but that of many others; some of birth as high as your own. He has the genius of riches, and knocks off a million as a poet does an ode, by the force of inspiration. He is hand-in-glove with the Ministers, and has been invited to Compiègne by the Emperor. You will find him very useful."

Alain made a slight movement of incredulous dissent, and changed the conversation to reminiscences of old schoolboy days.

The dinner at length came to a close. Frederic rang for the bill—glanced over it. "Fifty-nine francs," said he, carelessly flinging down his napoleon and a half. The Marquis silently drew forth his purse and extracted the same sum.

When they were out of the *restaurant*, Frederic proposed adjourning to his own rooms. "I can promise you an excellent cigar, one of a box given to me by an invaluable young Spaniard attached to the Embassy here. Such cigars are not to be had at Paris for money, nor even for love, seeing that women, however devoted and generous, never offer you anything better than a cigarette. Such cigars are only to be had for friendship. Friendship is a jewel."

"I never smoke," answered the Marquis, "but I shall be charmed to come to your rooms; only don't let me encroach on your good-nature. Doubtless you have engagements for the evening."

"None till eleven o'clock, when I have promised to go to a *soirée* to which I do not offer to take you; for it is one of those Bohemian entertainments at which it would do you harm in the Faubourg to assist—at least until you have made good your position. Let me see, is not the Duchesse de Tarascon a relation of yours?"

"Yes; my poor mother's first cousin."

"I congratulate you. *Très grande dame.* She will

launch you *in puro cœlo*, as Juno might have launched one of her young peacocks."

"There has been no acquaintance between our houses," returned the Marquis, drily, "since the *mésalliance* of her second nuptials."

"*Mésalliance!* second nuptials! Her second husband was the Duc de Tarascon."

"A duke of the First Empire—the grandson of a butcher."

"*Diable!* you are a severe genealogist, Monsieur le Marquis. How can you consent to walk arm-in-arm with me, whose great-grandfather supplied bread to the same army to which the Duc de Tarascon's grandfather furnished the meat?"

"My dear Frederic, we two have an equal pedigree, for our friendship dates from the same hour. I do not blame the Duchesse de Tarascon for marrying the grandson of a butcher, but for marrying the son of a man made duke by an usurper. She abandoned the faith of her house and the cause of her sovereign. Therefore her marriage is a blot on our scutcheon."

Frederic raised his eyebrows, but had the tact to pursue the subject no further. He who interferes in the quarrels of relations must pass through life without a friend.

The young men now arrived at Lemercier's apartment, an *entresol* looking on the Boulevard des Italiens, consisting of more rooms than a bachelor generally requires; low-pitched, indeed, but of good dimensions,

and decorated and furnished with a luxury which really
astonished the provincial, though, with the high-bred
pride of an oriental, he suppressed every sign of surprise.

Florentine cabinets freshly retouched by the exquisite
skill of Mombro, costly specimens of old Sèvres and
Limoges; pictures and bronzes and marble statuettes
—all well chosen and of great price, reflected from
mirrors in Venetian frames—made a *coup d'œil* very
favourable to that respect which the human mind pays
to the evidences of money. Nor was comfort less
studied than splendour. Thick carpets covered the
floors, doubled and quilted *portières* excluded all
draughts from chinks in the doors. Having allowed
his friend a few minutes to contemplate and admire
the *salle à manger* and *salon* which constituted his
more state apartments, Frederic then conducted him
into a small cabinet, fitted up with scarlet cloth and
gold fringes, whereon were artistically arranged trophies
of Eastern weapons and Turkish pipes with amber
mouthpieces.

There, placing the Marquis at ease on a divan and
flinging himself on another, the Parisian exquisite ordered a valet, well dressed as himself, to bring coffee
and liqueurs; and after vainly pressing one of his
matchless cigars on his friend, indulged in his own
Regalia.

"They are ten years old," said Frederic, with a
tone of compassion at Alain's self-inflicted loss—"ten

years old. Born therefore about the year in which we two parted——"

"When you were so hastily summoned from college," said the Marquis, "by the news of your father's illness. We expected you back in vain. Have you been at Paris ever since?"

"Ever since; my poor father died of that illness. His fortune proved much larger than was suspected— my share amounted to an income from investments in stocks, houses, &c., to upwards of 60,000 francs a-year; and as I wanted six years to my majority, of course the capital on attaining my majority would be increased by accumulation. My mother desired to keep me near her; my uncle, who was joint guardian with her, looked with disdain on our poor little provincial cottage; so promising an heir should acquire his finishing education under masters at Paris. Long before I was of age, I was initiated into politer mysteries of our capital than those celebrated by Eugene Sue. When I took possession of my fortune five years ago, I was considered a Crœsus; and really for that patriarchal time I was wealthy. Now, alas! my accumulations have vanished in my outfit; and 60,000 francs a-year is the least a Parisian can live upon. It is not only that all prices have fabulously increased, but that the dearer things become, the better people live. When I first came out, the world speculated upon me; now, in order to keep my standing, I am forced to speculate on the world. Hitherto I have not lost; Duplessis let me into a few good things this year, worth 100,000 francs or so.

Crœsus consulted the Delphic Oracle. Duplessis was not alive in the time of Crœsus, or Crœsus would have consulted Duplessis."

Here there was a ring at the outer door of the apartment, and in another minute the valet ushered in a gentleman somewhere about the age of thirty, of prepossessing countenance, and with the indefinable air of good-breeding and *usage du monde*. Frederic started up to greet cordially the new-comer, and introduced him to the Marquis under the name of "Sare Grarm Varn."

"Decidedly," said the visitor, as he took off his paletot and seated himself beside the Marquis—"decidedly, my dear Lemercier," said he, in very correct French, and with the true Parisian accent and intonation. "You Frenchmen merit that praise for polished ignorance of the language of barbarians which a distinguished historian bestows on the ancient Romans. Permit me, Marquis, to submit to you the consideration whether Grarm Varn is a fair rendering of my name as truthfully printed on this card."

The inscription on the card, thus drawn from its case and placed in Alain's hand, was—

MR GRAHAM VANE,
No. — Rue D'Anjou.

The Marquis gazed at it as he might on a hieroglyphic, and passed it on to Lemercier in discreet silence.

That gentleman made another attempt at the barbarian appellation.

"'Grür—häm Varne.' *C'est ça!* I triumph! all difficulties yield to French energy."

Here the coffee and liqueurs were served; and after a short pause the Englishman, who had very quietly been observing the silent Marquis, turned to him and said: "Monsieur le Marquis, I presume it was your father whom I remember as an acquaintance of my own father at Ems. It is many years ago; I was but a child. The Count de Chambord was then at that enervating little spa for the benefit of the Countess's health. If our friend Lemercier does not mangle your name as he does mine, I understand him to say that you are the Marquis de Rochebriant."

"That is my name: it pleases me to hear that my father was among those who flocked to Ems to do homage to the royal personage who deigns to assume the title of Count de Chambord."

"My own ancestors clung to the descendants of James II. till their claims were buried in the grave of the last Stuart; and I honour the gallant men who, like your father, revere in an exile the heir to their ancient kings."

The Englishman said this with grace and feeling; the Marquis's heart warmed to him at once.

"The first loyal *gentilhomme* I have met at Paris," thought the Legitimist; "and, oh, shame! not a Frenchman!"

Graham Vane, now stretching himself and accept-

ing the cigar which Lemercier offered him, said to
that gentleman: "You who know your Paris by heart
—everybody and everything therein worth the knowing, with many bodies and many things that are not
worth it—can you inform me who and what is a
certain lady who every fine day may be seen walking
in a quiet spot at the outskirts of the Bois de Boulogne,
not far from the Baron de Rothschild's villa? The
said lady arrives at this selected spot in a dark-blue
coupé without armorial bearings, punctually at the
hour of three. She wears always the same dress, a
kind of grey pearl-coloured silk, with a *cachemire*
shawl. In age she may be somewhat about twenty—
a year or so more or less—and has a face as haunting
as a Medusa's; not, however, a face to turn a man
into a stone, but rather of the two turn a stone into
a man. A clear paleness, with a bloom like an
alabaster lamp with the light flashing through. I
borrow that illustration from Sare Scott, who applied
it to Milor Bee-ron."

"I have not seen the lady you describe," answered
Lemercier, feeling humiliated by the avowal; "in fact,
I have not been in that sequestered part of the Bois
for months; but I will go to-morrow: three o'clock
you say—leave it to me; to-morrow evening, if she
is a Parisienne, you shall know all about her. But,
mon cher, you are not of a jealous temperament to
confide your discovery to another."

"Yes, I am of a very jealous temperament," replied
the Englishman; "but jealousy comes after love, and

not before it. I am not in love; I am only haunted.
To-morrow evening, then, shall we dine at Philippe's,
seven o'clock 1"

"With all my heart," said Lemercier; "and you
too, Alain."

"Thank you, no," said the Marquis, briefly; and
he rose, drew on his gloves, and took up his hat.

At these signals of departure, the Englishman,
who did not want tact nor delicacy, thought that he
had made himself *de trop* in the *tête-à-tête* of two
friends of the same age and nation; and, catching
up his paletot, said hastily, "No, Marquis, do not go
yet, and leave our host in solitude; for I have an
engagement which presses, and only looked in at
Lemercier's for a moment, seeing the light at his windows. Permit me to hope that our acquaintance will
not drop, and inform me where I may have the honour
to call on you."

"Nay," said the Marquis; "I claim the right of
a native to pay my respects first to the foreigner who
visits our capital, and," he added in a lower tone,
"who speaks so nobly of those who revere its exiles."

The Englishman saluted, and walked slowly towards the door; but on reaching the threshold turned
back and made a sign to Lemercier, unperceived by
Alain.

Frederic understood the sign, and followed Graham Vane into the adjoining room, closing the door
as he passed.

"My dear Lemercier, of course I should not have

intruded on you at this hour on a mere visit of ceremony. I called to say that the Mademoiselle Duval
whose address you sent me is not the right one—not
the lady whom, knowing your wide range of acquaintance, I asked you to aid me in finding out."

"Not the right Duval? *Diable!* she answered your
description exactly."

"Not at all."

"You said she was very pretty and young—under
twenty."

"You forgot that I said she deserved that description twenty-one years ago."

"Ah, so you did; but some ladies are always
young. 'Age,' says a wit in the *Figaro*, 'is a river
which the women compel to reascend to its source
when it has flowed onward more than twenty years.'
Never mind—*soyez tranquille*—I will find your Duval
yet if she is to be found. But why could not the
friend who commissioned you to inquire choose a
name less common? Duval! every street in Paris
has a shop-door over which is inscribed the name of
Duval."

"Quite true, there is the difficulty; however, my
dear Lemercier, pray continue to look out for a Louise
Duval who was young and pretty twenty-one years
ago—this search ought to interest me more than that
which I intrusted to you to-night, respecting the
pearly-robed lady: for in the last I but gratify my
own whim; in the first I discharge a promise to a
friend. You, so perfect a Frenchman, know the

difference; honour is engaged to the first. Be sure you let me know if you find any other Madame or Mademoiselle Duval; and of course you remember your promise not to mention to any one the commission of inquiry you so kindly undertake. I congratulate you on your friendship for M. de Rochebriant. What a noble countenance and manner!"

Lemercier returned to the Marquis. "Such a pity you can't dine with us to-morrow. I fear you made but a poor dinner to-day. But it is always better to arrange the *menu* beforehand. I will send to Philippe's to-morrow. Do not be afraid."

The Marquis paused a moment, and on his young face a proud struggle was visible. At last he said, bluntly and manfully—

"My dear Frederic, your world and mine are not and cannot be the same. Why should I be ashamed to own to my old schoolfellow that I am poor—very poor; that the dinner I have shared with you to-day is to me a criminal extravagance? I lodge in a single chamber on the fourth storey; I dine off a single *plat* at a small *restaurateur's;* the utmost income I can allow to myself does not exceed 5000 francs a-year: my fortunes I cannot hope much to improve. In his own country Alain de Rochebriant has no career."

Lemercier was so astonished by this confession that he remained for some moments silent, eyes and mouth both wide open; at length he sprang up, embraced his friend wellnigh sobbing, and exclaimed, "*Tant mieux pour moi!* You must take your lodging

with me. I have a charming bedroom to spare. Don't
say no. It will raise my own position to say 'I and
Rochebriant keep house together.' It must be so.
Come here to-morrow. As for not having a career
—bah! I and Duplessis will settle that. You shall be
a *millionnaire* in two years. Meanwhile we will join
capitals: I my paltry notes, you your grand name.
Settled!"

"My dear, dear Frederic," said the young noble,
deeply affected, "on reflection you will see what
you propose is impossible. Poor I may be without
dishonour; live at another man's cost I cannot do
without baseness. It does not require to be *gentil-
homme* to feel that: it is enough to be a Frenchman.
Come and see me when you can spare the time. There
is my address. You are the only man in Paris to
whom I shall be at home. *Au revoir*." And breaking
away from Lemercier's clasp, the Marquis hurried off.

———

CHAPTER III.

ALAIN reached the house in which he lodged. Externally a fine house, it had been the hotel of a great family in the old *régime*. On the first floor were still superb apartments, with ceilings painted by Le Brun, with walls on which the thick silks still seemed fresh. These rooms were occupied by a rich *agent de change;* but, like all such ancient palaces, the upper storeys were wretchedly defective even in the comforts which poor men demand nowadays: a back staircase, narrow, dirty, never lighted, dark as Erebus, led to the room occupied by the Marquis, which might be naturally occupied by a needy student or a virtuous *grisette*. But there was to him a charm in that old hotel, and the richest *locataire* therein was not treated with a respect so ceremonious as that which attended the lodger on the fourth storey. The porter and his wife were Bretons; they came from the village of Rochebriant; they had known Alain's parents in their young days; it was their kinsman who had recommended him to the hotel which they served: so, when he paused at the lodge for his key, which he had left there, the porter's wife was in waiting for his return, and insisted on lighting him up-stairs and seeing to his fire, for after a warm

3*

day the night had turned to that sharp biting cold which is more trying in Paris than even in London.

The old woman, running up the stairs before him, opened the door of his room, and busied herself at the fire. "Gently, my good Martha," said he, "that log suffices. I have been extravagant to-day, and must pinch for it."

"M. le Marquis jests," said the old woman, laughing.

"No, Martha; I am serious. I have sinned, but I shall reform. *Entre nous*, my dear friend, Paris is very dear when one sets one's foot out of doors: I must soon go back to Rochebriant."

"When M. le Marquis goes back to Rochebriant he must take with him a Madame la Marquise—some pretty angel with a suitable *dot*."

"A *dot* suitable to the ruins of Rochebriant would not suffice to repair them, Martha: give me my dressing-gown, and good-night."

"*Bon repos, M. le Marquis! beaux rêves, et bel avenir.*"

"*Bel avenir!*" murmured the young man bitterly, leaning his cheek on his hand; "what fortune fairer than the present can be mine? yet inaction in youth is more keenly felt than in age. How lightly I should endure poverty if it brought poverty's ennobling companion, Labour—denied to me! Well, well; I must go back to the old rock: on this ocean there is no sail, not even an oar, for me."

Alain de Rochebriant had not been reared to the

expectation of poverty. The only son of a father whose estates were large beyond those of most nobles in modern France, his destined heritage seemed not unsuitable to his illustrious birth. Educated at a provincial academy, he had been removed at the age of sixteen to Rochebriant, and lived there simply and lonelily enough, but still in a sort of feudal state, with an aunt, an elder and unmarried sister to his father.

His father he never saw but twice after leaving college. That brilliant *seigneur* visited France but rarely, for very brief intervals, residing wholly abroad. To him went all the revenues of Rochebriant save what sufficed for the *ménage* of his son and his sister. It was the cherished belief of these two loyal natures that the Marquis secretly devoted his fortune to the cause of the Bourbons—how, they knew not, though they often amused themselves by conjecturing; and the young man, as he grew up, nursed the hope that he should soon hear that the descendant of Henri Quatre had crossed the frontier on a white charger and hoisted the old gonfalon with its *fleur-de-lis*. Then, indeed, his own career would be opened, and the sword of the Kerouecs drawn from its sheath. Day after day he expected to hear of revolts, of which his noble father was doubtless the soul. But the Marquis, though a sincere Legitimist, was by no means an enthusiastic fanatic. He was simply a very proud, a very polished, a very luxurious, and, though not without the kind-liness and generosity which were common attributes of the old French *noblesse*, a very selfish *grand seigneur*.

Losing his wife (who died the first year of marriage in giving birth to Alain) while he was yet very young, he had lived a frank libertine life until he fell submissive under the despotic yoke of a Russian Princess, who, for some mysterious reason, never visited her own country and obstinately refused to reside in France. She was fond of travel, and moved yearly from London to Naples, Naples to Vienna, Berlin, Madrid, Seville, Carlsbad, Baden-Baden—anywhere for caprice or change, except Paris. This fair wanderer succeeded in chaining to herself the heart and the steps of the Marquis de Rochebriant.

She was very rich; she lived semi-royally. Hers was just the house in which it suited the Marquis to be the *enfant gâté*. I suspect that, cat-like, his attachment was rather to the house than to the person of his mistress. Not that he was domiciled with the Princess; that would have been somewhat too much against the proprieties, greatly too much against the Marquis's notions of his own dignity. He had his own carriage, his own apartments, his own *suite*, as became so grand a *seigneur*, and the lover of so grand a *dame*. His estates, mortgaged before he came to them, yielded no income sufficient for his wants; he mortgaged deeper and deeper, year after year, till he could mortgage them no more. He sold his hotel at Paris—he accepted without scruple his sister's fortune —he borrowed with equal *sang froid* the two hundred thousand francs which his son on coming of age inherited from his mother. Alain yielded that fortune to him without a murmur—nay, with pride; he thought it destined to go towards raising a regiment for the *fleur-de-lis*.

To do the Marquis justice, he was fully persuaded that he should shortly restore to his sister and son what he so recklessly took from them. He was engaged to be married to his Princess so soon as her own husband died. She had been separated from the Prince for many years, and every year it was said he could not last a year longer. But he completed the measure of his conjugal iniquities by continuing to live; and one day, by mistake, Death robbed the lady of the Marquis instead of the Prince.

This was an accident which the Marquis had never counted upon. He was still young enough to consider himself young; in fact, one principal reason for keeping Alain secluded in Bretagne was his reluctance to introduce into the world a son "as old as myself" he would say pathetically. The news of his death, which happened at Baden after a short attack of bronchitis caught in a supper *al fresco* at the old castle, was duly transmitted to Rochebriant by the Princess; and the shock to Alain and his aunt was the greater because they had seen so little of the departed that they regarded him as a heroic myth, an impersonation of ancient chivalry, condemning himself to voluntary exile rather than do homage to usurpers. But from their grief they were soon roused by the terrible doubt

whether Rochebriant could still be retained in the
family. Besides the mortgagees, creditors from half
the capitals in Europe sent in their claims; and all the
movable effects transmitted to Alain by his father's
confidential Italian valet, except sundry carriages and
horses which were sold at Baden for what they would
fetch, were a magnificent dressing-case, in the secret
drawer of which were some bank-notes amounting to
thirty thousand francs, and three large boxes contain-
ing the Marquis's correspondence, a few miniature
female portraits, and a great many locks of hair.

Wholly unprepared for the ruin that stared him in
the face, the young Marquis evinced the natural strength
of his character by the calmness with which he met
the danger, and the intelligence with which he calcu-
lated and reduced it.

By the help of the family notary in the neighbour-
ing town, he made himself master of his liabilities and
his means; and he found that, after paying all debts
and providing for the interest of the mortgages, a property which ought to have realised a rental of £10,000
a-year, yielded not more than £400. Nor was
even this margin safe, nor the property out of peril;
for the principal mortgagee, who was a capitalist in
Paris named Louvier, having had during the life of
the late Marquis more than once to wait for his half-
yearly interest longer than suited his patience—and
his patience was not enduring—plainly declared that
if the same delay recurred he should put his right of
seizure in force; and in France still more than in

England, bad seasons seriously affect the security of rents. To pay away £9600 a-year regularly out of £10,000, with the penalty of forfeiting the whole if not paid, whether crops may fail, farmers procrastinate, and timber fall in price, is to live with the sword of Damocles over one's head.

For two years and more, however, Alain met his difficulties with prudence and vigour; he retrenched the establishment hitherto kept at the chateau, resigned such rural pleasures as he had been accustomed to indulge, and lived like one of his petty farmers. But the risks of the future remained undiminished.

"There is but one way, Monsieur le Marquis," said the family notary, M. Hébert, "by which you can put your estate in comparative safety. Your father raised his mortgages from time to time, as he wanted money, and often at interest above the average market interest. You may add considerably to your income by consolidating all these mortgages into one at a lower percentage, and in so doing pay off this formidable mortgagee, M. Louvier, who, I shrewdly suspect, is bent upon becoming the proprietor of Rochebriant. Unfortunately those few portions of your land which were but lightly charged, and, lying contiguous to small proprietors, were coveted by them, and could be advantageously sold, are already gone to pay the debts of Monsieur the late Marquis. There are, however, two small farms which, bordering close on the town of S——, I think I could dispose of for building purposes at high rates; but these lands are covered by

Monsieur Louvier's general mortgage, and he has refused to release them, unless the whole debt be paid.
Were that debt therefore transferred to another mortgagee, we might stipulate for their exception, and in
so doing secure a sum of more than 100,000 francs,
which you could keep in reserve for a pressing or
unforeseen occasion, and make the nucleus of a capital
devoted to the gradual liquidation of the charges on
the estate. For with a little capital, Monsieur le Marquis, your rent-roll might be very greatly increased,
the forests and orchards improved, those meadows
round S—— drained and irrigated. Agriculture is
beginning to be understood in Bretagne, and your
estate would soon double its value in the hands of a
spirited capitalist. My advice to you, therefore, is to
go to Paris, employ a good *avoué*, practised in such
branch of his profession, to negotiate the consolidation of your mortgages upon terms that will enable
you to sell outlying portions, and so pay off the
charge by instalments agreed upon;—to see if some
safe company or rich individual can be found to
undertake for a term of years the management of your
forests, the draining of the S—— meadows, the super-
intendence of your fisheries, &c. They, it is true, will
monopolise the profits for many years—perhaps twenty;
but you are a young man; at the end of that time you
will re-enter on your estate with a rental so improved
that the mortgages, now so awful, will seem to you
comparatively trivial."

In pursuance of this advice, the young Marquis

had come to Paris fortified with a letter from M.
Hébert to an *avoué* of eminence, and with many letters from his aunt to the nobles of the Faubourg
connected with his house. Now one reason why
M. Hébert had urged his client to undertake this important business in person, rather than volunteer his own
services in Paris, was somewhat extra-professional. He
had a sincere and profound affection for Alain; he
felt compassion for that young life so barrenly wasted
in seclusion and severe privations; he respected, but
was too practical a man of business to share, those
chivalrous sentiments of loyalty to an exiled dynasty
which disqualified the man for the age he lived in,
and, if not greatly modified, would cut him off from
the hopes and aspirations of his eager generation. He
thought plausibly enough that the air of the grand
metropolis was necessary to the mental health, en-
feebled and withering amidst the feudal mists of
Bretagne; that once in Paris, Alain would imbibe the
ideas of Paris, adapt himself to some career leading
to honour and to fortune, for which he took facilities
from his high birth, an historical name too national
for any dynasty not to welcome among its adherents,
and an intellect not yet sharpened by contact and
competition with others, but in itself vigorous, habitu-
ated to thought, and vivified by the noble aspirations
which belong to imaginative natures.

At the least, Alain would be at Paris in the social
position which would afford him the opportunities of
a marriage, in which his birth and rank would be

readily accepted as an equivalent to some ample
fortune that would serve to redeem the endangered
seigneuries. He therefore warned Alain that the affair
for which he went to Paris might be tedious, that
lawyers were always slow, and advised him to cal-
culate on remaining several months, perhaps a year;
delicately suggesting that his rearing hitherto had
been too secluded for his age and rank, and that a
year at Paris, even if he failed in the object which
took him there, would not be thrown away in the
knowledge of men and things that would fit him better
to grapple with his difficulties on his return.

Alain divided his spare income between his aunt
and himself, and had come to Paris resolutely
determined to live within the £200 a-year which
remained to his share. He felt the revolution in his
whole being that commenced when out of sight of the
petty principality in which he was the object of that
feudal reverence, still surviving in the more unfre-
quented parts of Bretagne, for the representatives of
illustrious names connected with the immemorial
legends of the province.

The very bustle of a railway, with its crowd and
quickness and unceremonious democracy of travel,
served to pain and confound and humiliate that sense
of individual dignity in which he had been nurtured.
He felt that, once away from Rochebriant, he was but
a cipher in the sum of human beings. Arrived at
Paris, and reaching the gloomy hotel to which he had
been recommended, he greeted even the desolation of

that solitude which is usually so oppressive to a
stranger in the metropolis of his native land. Lone-
liness was better than the loss of self in the reek and
pressure of an unfamiliar throng. For the first few
days he had wandered over Paris without calling even
on the *avoué* to whom M. Hébert had directed him.
He felt with the instinctive acuteness of a mind which,
under sounder training, would have achieved no mean
distinction, that it was a safe precaution to imbue
himself with the atmosphere of the place, and seize
on those general ideas which in great capitals are so
contagious that they are often more accurately caught
by the first impressions than by subsequent habit, before he brought his mind into collision with those of
the individuals he had practically to deal with.

At last he repaired to the *avoué*, M. Gandrin, Rue
St. Florentin. He had mechanically formed his idea
of the abode and person of an *avoué* from his association with M. Hébert. He expected to find a dull
house in a dull street near the centre of business,
remote from the haunts of idlers, and a grave man of
unpretending exterior and matured years.

He arrived at a hotel newly fronted, richly decorated, in the fashionable *quartier* close by the Tuileries.
He entered a wide *porte cochère*, and was directed by
the *concierge* to mount *au premier*. There, first de-
tained in an office faultlessly neat, with spruce young
men at smart desks, he was at length admitted into a
noble *salon*, and into the presence of a gentleman
lounging in an easy-chair before a magnificent bureau

of *marqueterie, genre Louis Seize*, engaged in patting a white curly lap-dog, with a pointed nose and a shrill bark.

The gentleman rose politely on his entrance, and released the dog, who, after sniffing the Marquis, condescended not to bite.

"Monsieur le Marquis," said M. Gandrin, glancing at the card and the introductory note from M. Hébert, which Alain had sent in, and which lay on the *secrétaire* beside heaps of letters nicely arranged and labelled "charmed to make the honour of your acquaintance; just arrived at Paris? So M. Hébert—a very worthy person whom I have never seen, but with whom I have had correspondence—tells me you wish for my advice; in fact, he wrote to me some days ago, mentioning the business in question—consolidation of mortgages. A very large sum wanted, Monsieur le Marquis, and not to be had easily."

"Nevertheless," said Alain, quietly, "I should imagine that there must be many capitalists in Paris willing to invest in good securities at fair interest."

"You are mistaken, Marquis; very few such capitalists. Men worth money nowadays like quick returns and large profits, thanks to the magnificent system of *Crédit Mobilier*, in which, as you are aware, a man may place his money in any trade or speculation without liabilities beyond his share. Capitalists are nearly all traders or speculators."

"Then," said the Marquis, half rising. "I am to presume, sir, that you are not likely to assist me."

"No, I don't say that, Marquis. I will look with care into the matter. Doubtless you have with you an abstract of the necessary documents, the conditions of the present mortgages, the rental of the estate, its probable prospects, and so forth."

"Sir, I have such an abstract with me at Paris; and having gone into it myself with M. Hébert, I can pledge you my word that it is strictly faithful to the facts."

The Marquis said this with *naïve* simplicity, as if his word were quite sufficient to set that part of the question at rest.

M. Gandrin smiled politely and said, "*Eh bien*, M. le Marquis: favour me with the abstract; in a week's time you shall have my opinion. You enjoy Paris? Greatly improved under the Emperor. *A propos*, Madame Gandrin receives to-morrow evening; allow me that opportunity to present you to her."

Unprepared for the proffered hospitality, the Marquis had no option but to murmur his gratification and assent.

In a minute more he was in the streets. The next evening he went to Madame Gandrin's—a brilliant reception—a whole moving flower-bed of 'decorations' there. Having gone through the ceremony of presentation to Madame Gandrin—a handsome woman dressed to perfection, and conversing with the secretary to an embassy—the young noble ensconced himself in an obscure and quiet corner, observing all, and imagining that he escaped observation. And as the young men of his own years glided by him, or as their talk reached his ears, he became aware that from top to toe, within and without, he was old-fashioned, obsolete, not of his race, not of his day. His rank itself seemed to him a waste-paper title-deed to a heritage long lapsed. Not thus the princely *seigneurs* of Rochebriant made their *début* at the capital of their nation. They had had the *entrée* to the cabinets of their kings; they had glittered in the halls of Versailles; they had held high posts of distinction in court and camp; the great Order of St. Louis had seemed their hereditary appanage. His father, though a voluntary exile in manhood, had been in childhood a king's page, and throughout life remained the associate of princes; and here, in an *avoué's soirée*, unknown, unregarded, an expectant on an *avoué's* patronage, stood the last lord of Rochebriant.

It is easy to conceive that Alain did not stay long. But he stayed long enough to convince him that on £200 a-year the polite society of Paris, even as seen at M. Gandrin's, was not for him. Nevertheless, a day or two after, he resolved to call upon the nearest of his kinsmen to whom his aunt had given him letters. With the Count de Vandemar, one of his fellow-nobles of the sacred Faubourg, he should be no less Rochebriant, whether in a garret or a palace. The Vandemars, in fact, though for many generations before the First Revolution a puissant and brilliant family, had always recognised the Rochebriants as the head of their house—the trunk from which they had been

slipped in the fifteenth century, when a younger son
of the Rochebriants married a wealthy heiress and
took the title, with the lands, of Vandemar.

Since then the two families had often intermar-
ried. The present count had a reputation for ability,
was himself a large proprietor, and might furnish advice to guide Alain in his negotiations with M. Gandrin. The Hotel de Vandemar stood facing the old
Hotel de Rochebriant; it was less spacious, but not
less venerable, gloomy, and prison-like.

As he turned his eyes from the armorial scutcheon
which still rested, though chipped and mouldering, over
the portals of his lost ancestral house, and was about
to cross the street, two young men, who seemed two
or three years older than himself, emerged on horseback from the Hotel de Vandemar.

Handsome young men, with the lofty look of the
old race, dressed with the punctilious care of person
which is not foppery in men of birth, but seems part
of the self-respect that appertains to the old chivalric
point of honour. The horse of one of these cavaliers
made a caracole which brought it nearly upon Alain
as he was about to cross. The rider, checking his
steed, lifted his hat to Alain and uttered a word of
apology in the courtesy of ancient high-breeding, but
still with condescension as to an inferior. This little
incident, and the slighting kind of notice received
from coevals of his own birth, and doubtless his own
blood—for he divined truly that they were the sons
of the Count de Vandemar—disconcerted Alain to a

degree which perhaps a Frenchman alone can comprehend. He had even half a mind to give up his visit and turn back. However, his native manhood prevailed over that morbid sensitiveness which, born out of the union of pride and poverty, has all the effects of vanity, and yet is not vanity itself.

The Count was at home, a thin spare man with a narrow but high forehead, and an expression of countenance keen, severe, and *un peu moqueuse.*

He received the Marquis, however, at first with great cordiality, kissed him on both sides of his cheek, called him "cousin," expressed immeasurable regret that the Countess was gone out on one of the missions of charity in which the great ladies of the Faubourg religiously interest themselves, and that his sons had just ridden forth to the Bois.

As Alain, however, proceeded, simply and without false shame, to communicate the object of his visit at Paris, the extent of his liabilities, and the penury of his means, the smile vanished from the Count's face; he somewhat drew back his *fauteuil* in the movement common to men who wish to estrange themselves from some other man's difficulties; and when Alain came to a close, the Count remained some moments seized with a slight cough; and, gazing intently on the carpet, at length he said, "My dear young friend, your father behaved extremely ill to you—dishonourably, fraudulently."

"Hold!" said the Marquis, colouring high. "Those

are words no man can apply to my father in my presence."

The Count stared, shrugged his shoulders, and replied with *sang froid*—

"Marquis, if you are contented with your father's
conduct, of course it is no business of mine: he never
injured me. I presume, however, that, considering my
years and my character, you come to me for advice—
is it so?"

Alain bowed his head in assent.

"There are four courses for one in your position
to take," said the Count, placing the index of the
right hand successively on the thumb and three fingers
of the left—"four courses, and no more.

"1st. To do as your notary recommended: consolidate your mortgages, patch up your income as you
best can, return to Rochebriant, and devote the rest
of your existence to the preservation of your property.
By that course your life will be one of permanent
privation, severe struggle; and the probability is that
you will not succeed: there will come one or two bad
seasons, the farmers will fail to pay, the mortgagee
will foreclose, and you may find yourself, after twenty
years of anxiety and torment, prematurely old and
without a *sou*.

"Course the 2d. Rochebriant, though so heavily
encumbered as to yield you some such income as
your father gave to his *chef de cuisine*, is still one of
those superb *terres* which bankers and Jews and stock-
jobbers court and hunt after, for which they will give

4*

enormous sums. If you place it in good hands, I do
not doubt that you could dispose of the property
within three months, on terms that would leave you a
considerable surplus, which, invested with judgment,
would afford you whereon you could live at Paris in
a way suitable to your rank and age.—Need we go
further?—does this course smile to you?"

"Pass on, Count; I will defend to the last what I
take from my ancestors, and cannot voluntarily sell
their rooftree and their tombs."

"Your name would still remain, and you would
be just as well received in Paris, and your *noblesse*
just as implicitly conceded, if all Judæa encamped
upon Rochebriant. Consider how few of us *gentilshommes* of the old *régime* have any domains left to
us. Our names alone survive; no revolution can
efface *them*."

"It may be so, but pardon me; there are subjects
on which we cannot reason — we can but feel.
Rochebriant may be torn from me, but I cannot
yield it."

"I proceed to the third course. Keep the chateau
and give up its traditions; remain *de facto* Marquis of
Rochebriant, but accept the new order of things.
Make yourself known to the people in power. They
will be charmed to welcome you;—a convert from
the old *noblesse* is a guarantee of stability to the new
system. You will be placed in diplomacy; effloresce
into an ambassador, a minister—and ministers

nowadays have opportunities to become enormously rich."

"That course is not less impossible than the last. Till Henry V. formally resign his right to the throne of St. Louis, I can be servant to no other man seated on that throne."

"Such, too, is my creed," said the Count, "and I cling to it; but my estate is not mortgaged, and I have neither the tastes nor the age for public employments. The last course is perhaps better than the rest; at all events it is the easiest. A wealthy marriage; even if it must be a *mésalliance*. I think at your age, with your appearance, that your name is worth at least two million francs in the eyes of a rich *roturier* with an ambitious daughter."

"Alas!" said the young man, rising, "I see I shall have to go back to Rochebriant. I cannot sell my castle, I cannot sell my creed, and I cannot sell my name and myself."

"The last all of us did in the old *régime*, Marquis. Though I still retain the title of Vandemar, my property comes from the Farmer-General's daughter, whom my great-grandfather, happily for us, married in the days of Louis Quinze. Marriages with people of sense and rank have always been *mariages de convenance* in France. It is only in *le petit monde* that men having nothing marry girls having nothing, and I don't believe they are a bit the happier for it. On the contrary, the quarrels *de ménage* leading to frightful crimes appear by the '*Gazette des Tribunaux*' to be

chiefly found among those who do not sell themselves
at the altar."

The old Count said this with a grim *persiflage*.
He was a Voltairian.

Voltairianism deserted by the modern Liberals of
France has its chief cultivation nowadays among the
wits of the old *régime*. They pick up its light weapons
on the battle-field on which their fathers perished, and
re-feather against the *canaille* the shafts which had
been pointed against the *noblesse*.

"Adieu, Count," said Alain, rising; "I do not
thank you less for your advice because I have not the
wit to profit by it."

"*Au revoir*, my cousin; you will think better of it
when you have been a month or two at Paris. By the
way, my wife receives every Wednesday; consider our
house yours."

"Count, can I enter into the world which Madame la Comtesse receives, in the way that becomes my birth, on the income I take from my
fortune?"

The Count hesitated. "No," said he at last,
frankly; "not because you will be less welcome or
less respected, but because I see that you have all
the pride and sensitiveness of a *seigneur de province*.
Society would therefore give you pain, not pleasure.
More than this, I know by the remembrance of my
own youth, and the sad experience of my own sons,
that you would be irresistibly led into debt, and debt
in your circumstances would be the loss of Roche-

briant. No; I invite you to visit us. I offer you the
most select but not the most brilliant circles of Paris,
because my wife is religious, and frightens away the
birds of gay plumage with the scarecrows of priests
and bishops. But if you accept my invitation and my
offer, I am bound, as an old man of the world to a
young kinsman, to say that the chances are that you
will be ruined."

"I thank you, Count, for your candour; and I now
acknowledge that I have found a relation and a
guide," answered the Marquis, with a nobility of mien
that was not without a pathos which touched the hard
heart of the old man.

"Come at least whenever you want a sincere if a
rude friend;" and though he did not kiss his cousin's
cheek this time, he gave him, with more sincerity, a
parting shake of the hand.

And these made the principal events in Alain's
Paris life till he met Frederic Lemercier. Hitherto he
had received no definite answer from M. Gandrin, who
had postponed an interview, not having had leisure to
make himself master of all the details in the abstract
sent to him.

CHAPTER IV.

THE next day, towards the afternoon, Frederic Lemercier, somewhat breathless from the rapidity at
which he had ascended to so high an eminence, burst
into Alain's chamber.

"*Pr-r! mon cher;* what superb exercise for the
health—how it must strengthen the muscles and ex-
pand the chest! after this, who should shrink from
scaling Mont Blanc!—Well, well. I have been meditating on your business ever since we parted. But I
would fain know more of its details. You shall confide them to me as we drive through the Bois. My
coupé is below, and the day is beautiful—come."

To the young Marquis, the gaiety, the heartiness
of his college friend were a cordial. How different
from the dry counsels of the Count de Vandemar!
Hope, though vaguely, entered into his heart. Wil-
lingly he accepted Frederic's invitation, and the young
men were soon rapidly borne along the Champs Elysées.
As briefly as he could Alain described the state of his
affairs, the nature of his mortgages, and the result of
his interview with M. Gandrin.

Frederic listened attentively. "Then Gandrin has
given you as yet no answer!"

"None: but I have a note from him this morning asking me to call to-morrow."

"After you have seen him, decide on nothing—if he makes you any offer. Get back your abstract, or a copy of it, and confide it to me. Gandrin ought to help you; he transacts affairs in a large way. *Belle clientèle* among the *millionnaires.* But his clients expect fabulous profits, and so does he. As for your principal mortgagee, Louvier, you know, of course, who he is."

"No, except that M. Hébert told me that he was very rich."

"Rich! I should think so; one of the Kings of Finance. Ah! observe those young men on horseback."

Alain looked forth and recognised the two cavaliers whom he had conjectured to be the sons of the Count de Vandemar.

"Those *beaux garçons* are fair specimens of your Faubourg," said Frederic; "they would decline my acquaintance because my grandfather kept a shop, and they keep a shop between them."

"A shop! I am mistaken, then. Who are they?"

"Raoul and Enguerrand, sons of that mocker of man the Count de Vandemar."

"And they keep a shop! you are jesting."

"A shop at which you may buy gloves and perfumes, Rue de la Chaussée d'Antin. Of course they don't serve at the counter; they only invest their pocket-money in the speculation, and in so doing—treble at

least their pocket-money, buy their horses, and keep
their grooms."

"Is it possible! nobles of such birth! How shocked
the Count would be if he knew it!"

"Yes, very much shocked if he was supposed to know
it. But he is too wise a father not to give his sons
limited allowances and unlimited liberty, especially the
liberty to add to the allowances as they please. Look
again at them; no better riders and more affectionate
brothers since the date of Castor and Pollux. Their
tastes indeed differ: Raoul is religious and moral,
melancholy and dignified; Enguerrand is a lion of the
first water,—*élégant* to the tips of his nails. These
demigods are nevertheless very mild to mortals. Though
Enguerrand is the best pistol-shot in Paris, and Raoul
the best fencer, the first is so good-tempered that you
would be a brute to quarrel with him, the last so true
a Catholic, that if you quarrelled with him you need
fear not his sword. He would not die in the committal
of what the Church holds a mortal sin."

"Are you speaking ironically! Do you mean to
imply that men of the name of Vandemar are not
brave?"

"On the contrary, I believe that, though masters
of their weapons, they are too brave to abuse their
skill; and I must add, that though they are sleeping
partners in a shop, they would not cheat you of a
farthing.—Benign stars on earth, as Castor and Pollux
were in heaven."

"But partners in a shop!"

"Bah! when a minister himself, like the late M. de M——, kept a shop, and added the profits of *bon bons* to his revenue, you may form some idea of the spirit of the age. If young nobles are not generally sleeping partners in shops, still they are more or less adventurers in commerce. The *Bourse* is the profession of those who have no other profession. You have visited the *Bourse?*"

"No."

"No! this is just the hour. We have time yet for the Bois.—Coachman, drive to the *Bourse.*"

"The fact is," resumed Frederic, "that gambling is one of the wants of civilised men. The *rouge-et-noir* and *roulette* tables are forbidden—the hells closed; but the passion for making money without working for it must have its vent, and that vent is the *Bourse*. As instead of a hundred wax-lights you now have one jet of gas, so instead of a hundred hells you have now one *Bourse*, and—it is exceedingly convenient; always at hand; no discredit being seen there as it was to be seen at Frascati's,—on the contrary, at once respectable, and yet the *mode.*"

The *coupé* stops at the *Bourse*, our friends mount the steps, glide through the pillars, deposit their canes at a place destined to guard them, and the Marquis follows Frederic up a flight of stairs till he gains the open gallery round a vast hall below. Such a din! such a clamour! disputations, wrangling, wrathful.

Here Lemercier distinguished some friends, whom he joined for a few minutes.

Alain, left alone, looked down into the hall. He
thought himself in some stormy scene of the First Revolution. An English contested election in the market-
place of a borough when the candidates are running
close on each other, the result doubtful, passions excited, the whole borough in civil war, is peaceful
compared to the scene at the *Bourse.*

Bulls and bears screaming, bawling, gesticulating,
as if one were about to strangle the other; the whole,
to an uninitiated eye, a confusion, a Babel, which it
seems absolutely impossible to reconcile to the notion
of quiet mercantile transactions, the purchase and sale
of shares and stocks. As Alain gazed bewildered, he
felt himself gently touched, and, looking round, saw
the Englishman.

"A lively scene!" whispered Mr. Vane. "This is
the heart of Paris: it beats very loudly."

"Is your *Bourse* in London like this?"

"I cannot tell you; at our Exchange the general
public are not admitted; the privileged priests of that
temple sacrifice their victims in closed penetralia,
beyond which the sounds made in the operation do
not travel to ears profane. But had we an Exchange
like this open to all the world, and placed, not in a
region of our metropolis unknown to fashion, but in
some elegant square in St. James's or at Hyde Park
Corner, I suspect that our national character would
soon undergo a great change, and that all our idlers
and sporting-men would make their books there every
day, instead of waiting long months in *ennui* for the

Doncaster and the Derby. At present we have but few men on the turf; we should then have few men not on Exchange, especially if we adopt your law, and can contrive to be traders without risk of becoming bankrupts. Napoleon I. called us a shopkeeping nation. Napoleon III. has taught France to excel us in everything, and certainly he has made Paris a shopkeeping city."

Alain thought of Raoul and Enguerrand, and blushed to find that what he considered a blot on his countrymen was so familiarly perceptible to a foreigner's eye.

"And the Emperor has done wisely, at least for the time," continued the Englishman, with a more thoughtful accent. "He has found vent thus for that very dangerous class in Paris society to which the subdivision of property gave birth—viz., the crowd of well-born, daring young men without fortune and without profession. He has opened the *Bourse* and said, 'There, I give you employment, resource, an *avenir.*' He has cleared the byways into commerce and trade, and opened new avenues of wealth to the *noblesse,* whom the great Revolution so unwisely beggared. What other way to rebuild a *noblesse* in France, and give it a chance of power because an access to fortune? But to how many sides of your national character has the *Bourse* of Paris magnetic attraction! You Frenchmen are so brave that you could not be happy without facing danger, so covetous of distinction that you would pine yourselves away without a dash, *coûte que coûte,* at celebrity and a red ribbon. Danger! look below at that arena—there it is; danger daily, hourly. But there also is celebrity; win at the *Bourse*, as of old in a tournament, and paladins smile on you, and ladies give you their scarves, or, what is much the same, they allow you to buy their *cachemires*. Win at the *Bourse*—what follows? the Chamber, the Senate, the Cross, the Minister's *portefeuille*. I might rejoice in all this for the sake of Europe—could it last, and did it not bring the consequences that follow the demoralisation which attends it. The *Bourse* and the *Crédit Mobilier* keep Paris quiet—at least as quiet as it can be. These are the secrets of this reign of splendour; these the two *lions couchants* on which rests the throne of the Imperial reconstructor."

Alain listened surprised and struck. He had not given the Englishman credit for the cast of mind which such reflections evinced.

Here Lemercier rejoined them, and shook hands with Graham Vane, who, taking him aside, said, "But you promised to go to the Bois, and indulge my insane curiosity about the lady in the pearl-coloured robe?"

"I have not forgotten; it is not half-past two yet; you said three. *Soyez tranquille;* I drive thither from the *Bourse* with Rochebriant."

"Is it necessary to take with you that very good-looking Marquis?"

"I thought you said you were not jealous, because not yet in love. However, if Rochebriant occasions

you the pang which your humble servant failed to in-
flict, I will take care that he do not see the lady."

"No," said the Englishman; "on consideration, I
should be very much obliged to any one with whom
she would fall in love. That would disenchant me.
Take the Marquis by all means."

Meanwhile Alain, again looking down, saw just
under him, close by one of the pillars, Lucien Duplessis. He was standing apart from the throng—a
small space cleared round himself—and two men who
had the air of gentlemen of the *beau monde*, with whom he
was conferring. Duplessis, thus seen, was not like the
Duplessis at the *restaurant*. It would be difficult to
explain what the change was, but it forcibly struck
Alain: the air was more dignified, the expression
keener; there was a look of conscious power and
command about the man even at that distance; the
intense, concentrated intelligence of his eye, his firm
lip, his marked features, his projecting, massive brow,
—would have impressed a very ordinary observer. In
fact, the man was here in his native element—in the
field in which his intellect gloried, commanded, and
had signalised itself by successive triumphs. Just thus
may be the change in the great orator whom you
deemed insignificant in a drawing-room, when you see
his crest rise above a reverential audience; or the
great soldier, who was not distinguishable from the
subaltern in a peaceful club, could you see him issuing
the order to his aides-de-camp amidst the smoke and
roar of the battle-field.

"Ah, Marquis!" said Graham Vane, "are you gazing at Duplessis! He is the modern genius of Paris. · He is at once the Cousin, the Guizot, and the Victor Hugo of speculation. Philosophy—Eloquence —audacious Romance;—all Literature now is swallowed up in the sublime epic of *Agiotage*, and Duplessis is the poet of the Empire."

"Well said, M. Grarm Varn," cried Frederic, forgetting his recent lesson in English names. "Alain underrates that great man. How could an Englishman appreciate him so well."

"*Ma foi!*" returned Graham, quietly; "I am studying to think at Paris, in order some day or other to know how to act in London. Time for the Bois. Lemercier, we meet at seven—Philippe's."

CHAPTER V.

"WHAT do you think of the *Bourse?*" asked Le-mercier, as their carriage took the way to the Bois.

"I cannot think of it yet; I am stunned. It seems to me as if I had been at a *Sabbat*, of which the wizards were *agents de change*, but not less bent upon raising Satan."

"Pooh! the best way to exorcise Satan is to get rich enough not to be tempted by him. The fiend always loved to haunt empty places; and of all places nowa-days he prefers empty purses and empty stomachs."

"But do all people get rich at the *Bourse?* or is not one man's wealth many men's ruin?"

"That is a question not very easy to answer; but under our present system Paris gets rich, though at the expense of individual Parisians. I will try and explain. The average luxury is enormously increased even in my experience; what were once considered refinements and fopperies are now called necessary comforts. Prices are risen enormously,—house-rent doubled within the last five or six years; all articles of luxury are very much dearer; the very gloves I wear cost twenty per cent more than I used to pay for gloves of the same quality. How the people we meet live, and live so well, is an enigma that would defy

Œdipus if Œdipus were not a Parisian. But the main explanation is this: speculation and commerce, with the facilities given to all investments, have really opened more numerous and more rapid ways to fortune than were known a few years ago.

"Crowds are thus attracted to Paris, resolved to venture a small capital in the hope of a large one; they live on that capital, not on their income, as gamesters do. There is an idea among us that it is necessary to seem rich in order to become rich. Thus there is a general extravagance and profusion. English *milords* marvel at our splendour. Those who, while spending their capital as their income, fail in their schemes of fortune, after one, two, three, or four years—vanish. What becomes of them, I know no more than I do what becomes of the old moons. Their place is immediately supplied by new candidates. Paris is thus kept perennially sumptuous and splendid by the gold it engulfs. But then some men succeed— succeed prodigiously, preternaturally; they make colossal fortunes, which are magnificently expended. They set an example of show and pomp, which is of course the more contagious because so many men say, 'The other day those *millionnaires* were as poor as we are; they never economised; why should we?' Paris is thus doubly enriched—by the fortunes it swallows up, and by the fortunes it casts up; the last being always reproductive, and the first never lost except to the individuals."

"I understand; but what struck me forcibly at the

scene we have left was the number of young men there; young men whom I should judge by their appearance to be gentlemen, evidently not mere spectators—eager, anxious, with tablets in their hands. That old or middle-aged men should find a zest in the pursuit of gain I can understand, but youth and avarice seem to me a new combination, which Molière never divined in his '*Avare.*'"

"Young men, especially if young gentlemen, love pleasure; and pleasure in this city is very dear. This explains why so many young men frequent the *Bourse.* In the old gaming-tables now suppressed, young men were the majority; in the days of your chivalrous forefathers it was the young nobles, not the old, who would stake their very mantles and swords on a cast of the die. And naturally enough *mon cher;* for is not youth the season of hope, and is not hope the goddess of gaming, whether at *rouge et noir* or the *Bourse?*"

Alain felt himself more and more behind his generation. The acute reasoning of Lemercier humbled his *amour propre.* At college Lemercier was never considered Alain's equal in ability or book-learning. What a stride beyond his school-fellow had Lemercier now made! How dull and stupid the young provincial felt himself to be as compared with the easy cleverness and half-sportive philosophy of the Parisian's fluent talk!

He sighed with a melancholy and yet with a generous envy. He had too fine a natural perception not

to acknowledge that there is a rank of mind as well
as of birth, and in the first he felt that Lemercier
might well walk before a Rochebriant; but his very
humility was a proof that he underrated himself.

Lemercier did not excel him in mind, but in experience. And just as the drilled soldier seems a
much finer fellow than the raw recruit, because he
knows how to carry himself, but after a year's dis-
cipline the raw recruit may excel in martial air the
upright hero whom he now despairingly admires, and
never dreams he can rival; so set a mind from a
village into the drill of a capital, and see it a year
after; it may tower a head higher than its recruiting-
sergeant.

CHAPTER VL

"I BELIEVE," said Lemercier, as the *coupé* rolled through the lively alleys of the Bois de Boulogne, "that Paris is built on a loadstone, and that every Frenchman with some iron globules in his blood is irresistibly attracted towards it. The English never seem to feel for London the passionate devotion that we feel for Paris. On the contrary, the London middle class, the commercialists, the shopkeepers, the clerks, even the superior artisans compelled to do their business in the capital, seem always scheming and pining to have their home out of it, though but in a suburb."

"You have been in London, Frederic?"

"Of course; it is the *mode* to visit that dull and hideous metropolis."

"If it be dull and hideous, no wonder the people who are compelled to do business in it seek the pleasures of home out of it."

"It is very droll that though the middle class entirely govern the melancholy Albion, it is the only country in Europe in which the middle class seem to have no amusements; nay, they legislate against amusement. They have no leisure-day but Sunday; and on that day they close all their theatres, — even their

museums and picture-galleries. What amusements
there may be in England are for the higher classes
and the lowest."

"What are the amusements of the lowest class?"

"Getting drunk."

"Nothing else?"

"Yes. I was taken at night under protection of
a policeman to some *cabarets*, where I found crowds
of that class which is the stratum below the working
class; lads who sweep crossings and hold horses, men-
dicants, and, I was told, thieves, girls whom a servant-
maid would not speak to—very merry—dancing
quadrilles and waltzes, and regaling themselves on
sausages—the happiest-looking folks I found in all
London—and, I must say, conducting themselves very
decently.

"Ah!" Here Lemercier pulled the check-string.
"Will you object to a walk in this quiet alley? I
see some one whom I have promised the Englishman
to—— But heed me, Alain; don't fall in love with
her."

CHAPTER VIL

THE lady in the pearl-coloured dress! Certainly it was a face that might well arrest the eye and linger long on the remembrance.

There are certain "beauty-women" as there are certain "beauty-men," in whose features one detects no fault—who are the show-figures of any assembly in which they appear—but who, somehow or other, inspire no sentiment and excite no interest; they lack some expression, whether of mind or of soul, or of heart, without which the most beautiful face is but a beautiful picture. This lady was not one of those "beauty-women." Her features taken singly were by no means perfect, nor were they set off by any brilliancy of colouring. But the countenance aroused and impressed the imagination with a belief that there was some history attached to it which you longed to learn. The hair, simply parted over a forehead unusually spacious and high for a woman, was of lustrous darkness; the eyes, of a deep violet blue, were shaded with long lashes.

Their expression was soft and mournful, but unobservant. She did not notice Alain and Lemercier as the two men slowly passed her. She seemed abstracted, gazing into space as one absorbed in thought or reverie. Her complexion was clear and pale, and apparently betokened delicate health.

Lemercier seated himself on a bench beside the path, and invited Alain to do the same. "She will return this way soon," said the Parisian, "and we can observe her more attentively and more respectfully thus seated than if we were on foot; meanwhile, what do you think of her? Is she French—is she Italian? —can she be English?"

"I should have guessed Italian, judging by the darkness of the hair and the outline of the features; but do Italians have so delicate a fairness of complexion?"

"Very rarely; and I should guess her to be French, judging by the intelligence of her expression, the simple neatness of her dress, and by that nameless refinement of air in which a Parisienne excels all the descendants of Eve—if it were not for her eyes. I never saw a Frenchwoman with eyes of that peculiar shade of blue; and if a Frenchwoman had such eyes, I flatter myself she would have scarcely allowed us to pass without making some use of them."

"Do you think she is married?" asked Alain.

"I hope so—for a girl of her age, if *comme il faut*, can scarcely walk alone in the Bois, and would not have acquired that look so intelligent—more than intelligent—so poetic."

"But regard that air of unmistakable distinction, regard that expression of face—so pure, so virginal: *comme il faut* she must be."

As Alain said these last words, the lady, who had turned back, was approaching them, and in full view of their gaze. She seemed unconscious of their existence as before, and Lemercier noticed that her lips moved as if she were murmuring inaudibly to herself.

She did not return again, but continued her walk straight on till at the end of the alley she entered a carriage in waiting for her, and was driven off.

"Quick, quick!" cried Lemercier, running towards his own *coupé;* "we must give chase."

Alain followed somewhat less hurriedly, and, agreeably to instructions Lemercier had already given to his coachman, the Parisian's *coupé* set off at full speed in the track of the strange lady's, which was still in sight.

In less than twenty minutes the carriage in chase stopped at the *grille* of one of those charming little villas to be found in the pleasant suburb of A——; a porter emerged from the lodge, opened the gate; the carriage drove in, again stopped at the door of the house, and the two gentlemen could not catch even a glimpse of the lady's robe as she descended from the carriage and disappeared within the house.

"I see a *café* yonder," said Lemercier; "let us learn all we can as to the fair unknown, over a *sorbet* or a *petit verre.*"

Alain silently, but not reluctantly, consented. He felt in the fair stranger an interest new to his existence.

They entered the little *café*, and in a few minutes Lemercier, with the easy *savoir vivre* of a Parisian, had extracted from the *garçon* as much as probably any one in the neighbourhood knew of the inhabitants of the villa.

It had been hired and furnished about two months previously in the name of Signora Venosta; but according to the report of the servants, that lady appeared to be the *gouvernante* or guardian of a lady much younger, out of whose income the villa was rented and the household maintained.

It was for her the *coupé* was hired from Paris. The elder lady very rarely stirred out during the day, but always accompanied the younger in any evening visits to the theatre or the houses of friends.

It was only within the last few weeks that such visits had been made.

The younger lady was in delicate health, and under the care of an English physician famous for skill in the treatment of pulmonary complaints. It was by his advice that she took daily walking exercise in the Bois. The establishment consisted of three servants, all Italians, and speaking but imperfect French. The *garçon* did not know whether either of the ladies was married, but their mode of life was free from all scandal or suspicion; they probably belonged to the literary or musical world, as the *garçon* had observed as their visitors the eminent author M. Savarin and his wife; and, still more frequently, an old man not less eminent as a musical composer.

"It is clear to me now," said Lemercier, as the two friends reseated themselves in the carriage, "that our pearly *ange* is some Italian singer of repute enough in her own country to have gained already a competence; and that, perhaps on account of her own health or her friend's, she is living quietly here in the expectation of some professional engagement, or the absence of some foreign lover."

"Lover! do you think that?" exclaimed Alain, in a tone of voice that betrayed pain.

"It is possible enough; and in that case the Englishman may profit little by the information I have promised to give him."

"You have promised the Englishman?"

"Do you not remember last night that he described the lady, and said that her face haunted him: and I——"

"Ah! I remember now. What do you know of this Englishman? He is rich, I suppose."

"Yes, I hear he is very rich now; that an uncle lately left him an enormous sum of money. He was attached to the English Embassy many years ago, which accounts for his good French and his knowledge of Parisian life. He comes to Paris very often, and I have known him some time. Indeed he has intrusted to me a difficult and delicate commission. The English tell me that his father was one of the most eminent members of their Parliament, of ancient birth, very highly connected, but ran out his fortune and died poor; that our friend had for some years to maintain himself, I fancy, by his pen; that he is considered very able; and, now that his uncle has enriched him, likely to enter public life and run a career as distinguished as his father's."

"Happy man! happy are the English," said the Marquis, with a sigh; and as the carriage now entered Paris, he pleaded the excuse of an engagement, bade his friend good-bye, and went his way musing through the crowded streets.

CHAPTER VIII.

LETTER FROM ISAURA CICOGNA TO MADAME DE GRANTMESNIL.

VILLA D'——, A . . . . .

I CAN never express to you, my beloved Eulalie, the strange charm which a letter from you throws over my poor little lonely world for days after it is received. There is always in it something that comforts, something that sustains, but also a something that troubles and disquiets me. I suppose Goethe is right, "that it is the property of true genius to disturb all settled ideas," in order, no doubt, to lift them into a higher level when they settle down again.

Your sketch of the new work you are meditating amid the orange-groves of Provence interests me intensely; yet, do you forgive me when I add that the interest is not without terror. I do not find myself able to comprehend how, amid those lovely scenes of nature, your mind voluntarily surrounds itself with images of pain and discord. I stand in awe of the calm with which you subject to your analysis the infirmities of reason and the tumults of passion. And all those laws of the social state which seem to me so fixed and immovable you treat with so quiet a scorn, as if they were but the gossamer threads which a touch of your slight woman's hand could brush away. But I cannot venture to discuss such subjects with you. It is only the skilled enchanter who can stand safely in the magic circle, and compel the spirits that he summons, even if they are evil, to minister to ends in which he foresees a good.

We continue to live here very quietly, and I do not as yet feel the worse for the colder climate. Indeed, my wonderful doctor, who was recommended to me as American, but is in reality English, assures me that a single winter spent here under his care will suffice for my complete re-establishment. Yet that career, to the training for which so many years have been devoted, does not seem to me so alluring as it once did.

I have much to say on this subject, which I defer till I can better collect my own thoughts on it—at present they are confused and struggling. The great *Maestro* has been most gracious.

In what a radiant atmosphere his genius lives and breathes! Even in his cynical moods, his very cynicism has in it the ring of a jocund music—the laugh of Figaro, not of Mephistopheles.

We went to dine with him last week; he invited to meet us Madame S——, who has this year conquered all opposition, and reigns alone, the great S——. Mr. T——, a pianist of admirable promise—your friend M. Savarin, wit, critic, and poet, with his pleasant sensible wife, and a few others whom the

Maestro confided to me in a whisper, were authorities
in the press. After dinner S—— sang to us, magnificently, of course. Then she herself graciously
turned to me, said how much she had heard from the
Maestro in my praise, and so-and-so. I was persuaded
to sing after her. I need not say to what disadvantage.
But I forgot my nervousness; I forgot my audience; I
forgot myself, as I always do when once my soul, as
it were, finds wing in music, and buoys itself in air,
relieved from the sense of earth. I knew not that I
had succeeded till I came to a close, and then my
eyes resting on the face of the grand *prima donna*, I
was seized with an indescribable sadness—with a keen
pang of remorse. Perfect *artiste* though she be, and
with powers in her own realm of art which admit of
no living equal, I saw at once that I had pained her;
she had grown almost livid; her lips were quivering,
and it was only with a great effort that she muttered
out some faint words intended for applause. I com-
prehended by an instinct how gradually there can
grow upon the mind of an artist the most generous
that jealousy which makes the fear of a rival annihilate
the delight in art. If ever I should achieve S——'s
fame as a singer, should I feel the same jealousy? I
think not now, but I have not been tested. She went
away abruptly. I spare you the recital of the compliments paid to me by my other auditors, compliments
that gave me no pleasure; for on all lips, except those
of the *Maestro*, they implied, as the height of eulogy,
that I had inflicted torture upon S——. "If so," said

he, "she would be as foolish as a rose that was jealous
of the whiteness of a lily. You would do yourself
great wrong, my child, if you tried to vie with the
rose in its own colour."

He patted my bended head as he spoke, with that
kind of fatherly king-like fondness with which he
honours me; and I took his hand in mine, and kissed
it gratefully. "Nevertheless," said Savarin, "when the
lily comes out there will be a furious attack on it,
made by the clique that devotes itself to the rose: a
lily clique will be formed *en revanche*, and I foresee a
fierce paper war. Do not be frightened at its first
outburst; every fame worth having must be fought
for."

Is it so? have you had to fight for your fame,
Eulalie? and do you hate all contests as much as I do?

Our only other gaiety since I last wrote was a
soirée at M. Louvier's. That republican *millionnaire*
was not slow in attending to the kind letter you addressed to him recommending us to his civilities. He
called at once, placed his good offices at our disposal, took charge of my modest fortune, which he has
invested, no doubt, as safely as it is advantageously
in point of interest, hired our carriage for us, and in
short has been most amiably useful.

At his house we met many to me most pleasant,
for they spoke with such genuine appreciation of your
works and yourself. But there were others whom I
should never have expected to meet under the roof
of a Crœsus who has so great a stake in the order of

things established. One young man—a noble whom he specially presented to me, as a politician who would be at the head of affairs when the Red Republic was established—asked me whether I did not agree with him that all private property was public spoliation, and that the great enemy to civilisation was religion, no matter in what form.

He addressed to me these tremendous questions with an effeminate lisp, and harangued on them with small feeble gesticulations of pale dainty fingers covered with rings.

I asked him if there were many who in France shared his ideas.

"Quite enough to carry them some day," he answered, with a lofty smile. "And the day may be nearer than the world thinks, when my *confrères* will be so numerous that they will have to shoot down each other for the sake of cheese to their bread."

That day nearer than the world thinks! Certainly, so far as one may judge the outward signs of the world at Paris, it does not think of such things at all. With what an air of self-content the beautiful city parades her riches! Who can gaze on her splendid palaces, her gorgeous shops, and believe that she will give ear to doctrines that would annihilate private rights of property; or who can enter her crowded churches, and dream that she can ever again instal a republic too civilised for religion?

Adieu. Excuse me for this dull letter. If I have, written on much that has little interest even for me,

it is that I wish to distract my mind from brooding
over the question that interests me most, and on which
I most need your counsel. I will try to approach it
in my next.   ISAURA.

From the Same to the Same.

Eulalie, Eulalie!—What mocking spirit has been
permitted in this modern age of ours to place in the
heart of woman the ambition which is the prerogative
of men?—You indeed, so richly endowed with a man's
genius, have a right to man's aspirations. But what
can justify such ambition in me? Nothing but this
one unintellectual perishable gift of a voice that does·
but please in uttering the thoughts of others. Doubtless I could make a name familiar for its brief time to
the talk of Europe—a name, what name? a singer's
name. Once I thought that name a glory. Shall I
ever forget the day when you first shone upon me;
when, emerging from childhood as from a dim and
solitary bypath, I stood forlorn on the great thoroughfare of life, and all the prospects before me stretched
sad in mists and in rain? You beamed on me then
as the sun coming out from the cloud and changing
the face of earth; you opened to my sight the fairy-
land of poetry and art; you took me by the hand and
said, "Courage! there is at each step some green gap
in the hedgerows, some soft escape from the stony
thoroughfare. Beside the real life expands the ideal
life to those who seek it. Droop not, seek it; the
ideal life has its sorrows, but it never admits despair;'

as on the ear of him who follows the winding course of a stream, the stream ever varies the note of its music, now loud with the rush of the falls; now low and calm as it glides by the level marge of smooth banks; now sighing through the stir of the reeds; now babbling with a fretful joy as some sudden curve on the shore stays its flight among gleaming pebbles;—so to the soul of the artist is the voice of the art ever fleeting beside and before him. Nature gave thee the bird's gift of song—raise the gift into art, and make the art thy companion.

"Art and Hope were twin-born, and they die together."

See how faithfully I remember, methinks, your very words. But the magic of the words, which I then but dimly understood, was in your smile and in your eye, and the queen-like wave of your hand as if beckoning to a world which lay before you, visible and familiar as your native land. And how devotedly, with what earnestness of passion, I gave myself up to the task of raising my gift into an art! I thought of nothing else, dreamed of nothing else; and oh, how sweet to me then were words of praise! "Another year yet," at length said the masters, "and you ascend your throne among the queens of song." Then—then—I would have changed for no other throne on earth my hope of that to be achieved in the realms of my art. And then came that long fever: my strength broke down, and the *Maestro* said, "Rest, or your voice is gone, and your throne is lost for ever." How hateful that

rest seemed to me! You again came to my aid. You
said, "The time you think lost should be but time
improved. Penetrate your mind with other songs than
the trash of *Libretti.* The more you habituate yourself to the forms, the more you imbue yourself with
the spirit, in which passions have been expressed and
character delineated by great writers, the more completely you will accomplish yourself in your own
special art of singer and actress." So, then, you
allured me to a new study. Ah! in so doing did you
dream that you diverted me from the old ambition?
My knowledge of French and Italian, and my rearing
in childhood, which had made English familiar to me,
gave me the keys to the treasure-houses of three lan-
guages. Naturally I began with that in which your
master-pieces are composed. Till then I had not even
read your works. They were the first I chose. How
they impressed, how they startled me! what depths in
the mind of man, in the heart of woman, they revealed
to me! But I owned to you then, and I repeat it
now, neither they nor any of the works in romance
and poetry which form the boast of recent French
literature, satisfied yearnings for that calm sense of
beauty, that divine joy in a world beyond this world,
which you had led me to believe it was the prerogative
of ideal art to bestow. And when I told you this with
the rude frankness you had bid me exercise in talk
with you, a thoughtful melancholy shade fell over
your face, and you said quietly, "You are right, child;
we, the French of our time, are the offspring of revolu-

tions that settled nothing, unsettled all: we resemble
those troubled States which rush into war abroad in
order to re-establish peace at home. Our books suggest problems to men for reconstructing some social
system in which the calm that belongs to art may be
found at last: but such books should not be in your
hands; they are not for the innocence and youth of
women, as yet unchanged by the systems which exist."
And the next day you brought me Tasso's great poem,
the *Gerusalemme Liberata*, and said, smiling, "Art in
its calm is here."

You remember that I was then at Sorrento by the
order of my physician. Never shall I forget the soft
autumn day when I sat amongst the lonely rocklets to
the left of the town—the sea before me, with scarce a
ripple; my very heart steeped in the melodies of that
poem, so marvellous for a strength disguised in sweetness, and for a symmetry in which each proportion
blends into the other with the perfectness of a Grecian
statue. The whole place seemed to me filled with the
presence of the poet to whom it had given birth.
Certainly the reading of that poem formed an era in
my existence; to this day I cannot acknowledge the
faults or weaknesses which your criticisms pointed out
—I believe because they are in unison with my own
nature, which yearns for harmony, and, finding that,
rests contented. I shrink from violent contrasts, and
can discover nothing tame and insipid in a continu-
ance of sweetness and serenity. But it was not till
after I had read *La Gerusalemme* again and again,

and then sat and brooded over it, that I recognised
the main charm of the poem in the religion which
clings to it as the perfume clings to a flower—a religion sometimes melancholy, but never to me sad.
Hope always pervades it. Surely if, as you said,
"Hope is twin-born with art," it is because art at its
highest blends itself unconsciously with religion, and
proclaims its affinity with hope by its faith in some
future good more perfect than it has realised in the past.

Be this as it may, it was in this poem so pre-
eminently Christian that I found the something which
I missed and craved for in modern French masterpieces, even yours—a something spiritual, speaking to
my own soul, calling it forth; distinguishing it as an
essence apart from mere human reason; soothing, even
when it excited; making earth nearer to heaven. And
when I ran on in this strain to you after my own wild
fashion, you took my head between your hands and
kissed me, and said, "Happy are those who believe!
long may that happiness be thine!" Why did I not
feel in Dante the Christian charm that I felt in Tasso?
Dante in your eyes, as in those of most judges, is in-
finitely the greater genius, but reflected on the dark
stream of that genius the stars are so troubled, the
heaven so threatening.

Just as my year of holiday was expiring I turned
to English literature; and Shakespeare, of course, was
the first English poet put into my hands. It proves
how childlike my mind still was, that my earliest sensation in reading him was that of disappointment. It

was not only that, despite my familiarity with English (thanks chiefly to the care of him whom I call my second father), there is much in the metaphorical diction of Shakespeare which I failed to comprehend; but he seemed to me so far like the modern French writers who affect to have found inspiration in his muse, that he obtrudes images of pain and suffering without cause or motive sufficiently clear to ordinary understandings, as I had taught myself to think it ought to be in the drama.

He makes Fate so cruel that we lose sight of the mild deity behind her. Compare, in this, Corneille's '*Polyeucte*' with the 'Hamlet.' In the first an equal calamity befalls the good, but in their calamity they are blessed. The death of the martyr is the triumph of his creed. But when we have put down the English tragedy—when Hamlet and Ophelia are confounded in death with Polonius and the fratricidal king, we see not what good end for humanity is achieved. The passages that fasten on our memory do not make us happier and holier; they suggest but terrible problems, to which they give us no solution.

In the '*Horaces*' of Corneille there are fierce contests, rude passions, tears drawn from some of the bitterest sources of human pity; but then through all stands out, large and visible to the eyes of all spectators, the great ideal of devoted patriotism. How much of all that has been grandest in the life of France, redeeming even its worst crimes of revolution in the love of country, has had its origin in the '*Hor-*

aces' of Corneille. But I doubt if the fates of Corio-
lanus, and Cæsar, and Brutus, and Antony, in the
giant tragedies of Shakespeare, have made Englishmen
more willing to die for England. In fine, it was long
before—I will not say I understood or rightly appre-
ciated Shakespeare, for no Englishman would admit
that I or even you could ever do so,—but before I
could recognise the justice of the place his country
claims for him as the genius without an equal in the
literature of Europe. Meanwhile the ardour I had
put into study, and the wear and tear of the emotions
which the study called forth, made themselves felt in
a return of my former illness, with symptoms still more
alarming; and when the year was out I was ordained
to rest for perhaps another year before I could sing
in public, still less appear on the stage. How I rejoiced when I heard that fiat! for I emerged from that
year of study with a heart utterly estranged from the
profession in which I had centred my hopes before——.
Yes, Eulalie, you had bid me accomplish myself for
the arts of utterance by the study of arts in which
thoughts originate the words they employ; and in
doing so—I had changed myself into another being.
I was forbidden all fatigue of mind; my books were
banished, but not the new self which the books had
formed. Recovering slowly through the summer, I
came hither two months since, ostensibly for the advice of Dr. C——, but really in the desire to commune
with my own heart, and be still.

And now I have poured forth that heart to you—

would you persuade me still to be a singer? If you
do, remember at least how jealous and absorbing the
art of the singer and of the actress is. How completely I must surrender myself to it, and live among
books, or among dreams, no more. Can I be anything else but singer? and if not, should I be contented merely to read and to dream?

I must confide to you one ambition which during
the lazy Italian summer took possession of me—I must
tell you the ambition, and add that I have renounced
it as a vain one. I had hoped that I could compose,
I mean in music. I was pleased with some things I
did—they expressed in music what I could not express in words; and one secret object in coming here
was to submit them to the great *Maestro*. He listened
to them patiently; he complimented me on my accuracy in the mechanical laws of composition; he even
said that my favourite airs were "*touchants et gra-
cieux*."

And so he would have left me, but I stopped him
timidly, and said, "Tell me frankly, do you think that
with time and study I could compose music such as
singers equal to myself would sing to?"

"You mean as a professional composer?"

"Well, yes."

"And to the abandonment of your vocation as a
singer?"

"Yes."

"My dear child, I should be your worst enemy
if I encouraged such a notion; cling to the career in

which you can be greatest; gain but health, and I
wager my reputation on your glorious success on the
stage. What can you be as a composer? You will
set pretty music to pretty words, and will be sung in
drawing-rooms with the fame a little more or less that
generally attends the compositions of female amateurs.
Aim at something higher, as I know you would do,
and you will not succeed. Is there any instance in
modern times, perhaps in any times, of a female composer who attains even to the eminence of a third-rate
opera writer? Composition in letters may be of no
sex. In that Madame Dudevant and your friend Madame de Grantmesnil can beat most men; but the
genius of musical composition is *homme*, and accept
it as a compliment when I say that you are essentially
femme."

He left me, of course, mortified and humbled; but
I feel he is right as regards myself, though whether in
his depreciation of our whole sex I cannot say. But
as this hope has left me, I have become more dis-
quieted, still more restless. Counsel me, Eulalie;
counsel, and, if possible, comfort me.

ISAURA.

From the Same to the Same.

No letter from you yet, and I have left you in
peace for ten days. How do you think I have spent
them? The *Maestro* called on us with M. Savarin, to
insist on our accompanying them on a round of the
theatres. I had not been to one since my arrival. I

divined that the kind-hearted composer had a motive in this invitation. He thought that in witnessing the applauses bestowed on actors, and sharing in the fascination in which theatrical illusion holds an audience, my old passion for the stage, and with it the longing for an *artiste's* fame, would revive.

In my heart I wished that his expectations might be realised. Well for me if I could once more concentre all my aspirations on a prize within my reach!

We went first to see a comedy greatly in vogue, and the author thoroughly understands the French stage of our day. The acting was excellent in its way. The next night we went to the *Odéon*, a romantic melodrama in six acts, and I know not how many *tableaux*. I found no fault with the acting there. I do not give you the rest of our programme. We visited all the principal theatres, reserving the opera and Madame S—— for the last. Before I speak of the opera, let me say a word or two on the plays.

There is no country in which the theatre has so great a hold on the public as in France; no country in which the successful dramatist has so high a fame; no country perhaps in which the state of the stage so faithfully represents the moral and intellectual condition of the people. I say this not, of course, from my experience of countries which I have not visited, but from all I hear of the stage in Germany and in England.

The impression left on my mind by the perform-

ances I witnessed is, that the French people are becoming dwarfed. The comedies that please them are
but pleasant caricatures of petty sections in a corrupt
society. They contain no large types of human nature;
their witticisms convey no luminous flashes of truth;
their sentiment is not pure and noble—it is a sickly
and false perversion of the impure and ignoble into
travesties of the pure and noble.

Their melodramas cannot be classed as literature
—all that really remains of the old French genius is
its *vaudeville*.

Great dramatists create great parts. One great
part, such as a Rachel would gladly have accepted, I
have not seen in the dramas of the young generation.

High art has taken refuge in the opera; but that
is not French opera. I do not complain so much that
French taste is less refined. I complain that French
intellect is lowered. The descent from Polyeucte to
Ruy Blas is great, not so much in the poetry of form
as in the elevation of thought; but the descent from
Ruy Blas to the best drama now produced is out of
poetry altogether, and into those flats of prose which
give not even the glimpse of a mountain-top.

But now to the opera. S—— in Normal The
house was crowded, and its enthusiasm as loud as it
was genuine. You tell me that S—— never rivalled
Pasta, but certainly her Norma is a great performance.
Her voice has lost less of its freshness than I had been
told, and what is lost of it her practised management
conceals or carries off.

The *Maestro* was quite right—I could never vie with her in her own line; but conceited and vain as I may seem even to you in saying so, I feel in my own line that I could command as large an applause. —of course taking into account my brief-lived advantage of youth. Her acting, apart from her voice, does not please me. It seems to me to want intelligence of the subtler feelings, the under-current of emotion which constitutes the chief beauty of the situation and the character. Am I jealous when I say this? Read on and judge.

On our return that night, when I had seen the Venosta to bed, I went into my own room, opened the window, and looked out. A lovely night, mild as in spring at Florence—the moon at her full, and the stars looking so calm and so high beyond our reach of their tranquillity. The evergreens in the gardens of the villas around me silvered over, and the summer boughs, not yet clothed with leaves, were scarcely visible amid the changeless smile of the laurels. At the distance lay Paris, only to be known by its innumerable lights. And then I said to myself—

"No, I cannot be an actress; I cannot resign my real self for that vamped-up hypocrite before the lamps. Out on those stage-robes and painted cheeks! Out on that simulated utterance of sentiments learned by rote and practised before the looking-glass till every gesture has its drill!"

Then I gazed on those stars which provoke our questionings, and return no answer, till my heart grew full, so full, and I bowed my head and wept like a child.

From the Same to the Same.

And still no letter from you! I see in the journals that you have left Nice. Is it that you are too absorbed in your work to have leisure to write to me? I know you are not ill; for if you were, all Paris would know of it. All Europe has an interest in your health. Positively I will write to you no more till a word from yourself bids me do so.

I fear I must give up my solitary walks in the Bois de Boulogne: they were very dear to me, partly because the quiet path to which I confined myself was that to which you directed me as the one you habitually selected when at Paris, and in which you had brooded over and revolved the loveliest of your romances; and partly because it was there that, catching, alas! not inspiration but enthusiasm from the genius that had hallowed the place, and dreaming I might originate music, I nursed my own aspirations and murmured my own airs. And though so close to that world of Paris to which all artists must appeal for judgment or audience, the spot was so undisturbed, so sequestered. But of late that path has lost its solitude, and therefore its charm.

Six days ago the first person I encountered in my walk was a man whom I did not then heed. He seemed in thought, or rather in reverie, like myself; we passed each other twice or thrice, and I did not

notice whether he was young or old, tall or short; but
he came the next day, and a third day, and then I
saw that he was young, and, in so regarding him, his
eyes became fixed on mine. The fourth day he did
not come, but two other men came, and the look of
one was inquisitive and offensive. They sat themselves down on a bench in the walk, and though I
did not seem to notice them, I hastened home; and
the next day, in talking with our kind Madame Savarin,
and alluding to these quiet walks of mine, she hinted,
with the delicacy which is her characteristic, that the
customs of Paris did not allow Demoiselles *comme
il faut* to walk alone even in the most sequestered
paths of the Bois.

I begin now to comprehend your disdain of customs which impose chains so idly galling on the liberty
of our sex.

We dined with the Savarins last evening: what a
joyous nature he has! Not reading Latin, I only know
Horace by translations, which I am told are bad; but
Savarin seems to me a sort of half Horace. Horace
on his town-bred side, so playfully well-bred, so good-
humoured in his philosophy, so affectionate to friends,
and so biting to foes. But certainly Savarin could
not have lived in a country farm upon endives and
mallows. He is town-bred and Parisian, *jusqu'au bout
des ongles*. How he admires you, and how I love him
for it! Only in one thing he disappoints me there.
It is your style that he chiefly praises: certainly that
style is matchless; but style is only the clothing of

thought, and to praise your style seems to me almost
as invidious as the compliment to some perfect
beauty, not on her form and face, but on her taste
and dress.

We met at dinner an American and his wife—a
Colonel and Mrs. Morley: she is delicately handsome,
as the American women I have seen generally are,
and with that frank vivacity of manner which distinguishes them from English women. She seemed
to take a fancy to me, and we soon grew very good
friends.

She is the first advocate I have met, except yourself, of that doctrine upon the rights of Women—of
which one reads more in the journals than one hears
discussed in *salons*.

Naturally enough I felt great interest in that subject, more especially since my rambles in the Bois were
forbidden; and as long as she declaimed on the hard
fate of the women who, feeling within them powers
that struggle for air and light beyond the close pre-
cinct of household duties, find themselves restricted
from fair rivalry with men in such fields of knowledge
and toil and glory, as men since the world began have
appropriated to themselves, I need not say that I went
with her cordially: you can guess that by my former
letters. But when she entered into the detailed cata-
logue of our exact wrongs and our exact rights, I felt
all the pusillanimity of my sex, and shrank back in
terror.

Her husband, joining us when she was in full tide

of eloquence, smiled at me with a kind of saturnine mirth. "Mademoiselle, don't believe a word she says; it is only tall talk! In America the women are absolute tyrants, and it is I who, in concert with my oppressed countrymen, am going in for a platform agitation to restore the Rights of Men."

Upon this there was a lively battle of words between the spouses, in which, I must own, I thought the lady was decidedly worsted.

No, Eulalie, I see nothing in these schemes for altering our relations towards the other sex which would improve our condition. The inequalities we suffer are not imposed by law—not even by convention; they are imposed by nature.

Eulalie, you have had an experience unknown to me; you have loved. In that day did you—you, round whom poets and sages and statesmen gather, listening to your words as to an oracle—did you feel that your pride of genius had gone out from you—that your ambition lived in him whom you loved—that his smile was more to you than the applause of a world?

I feel as if love in a woman must destroy her rights of equality—that it gives to her a sovereign even in one who would be inferior to herself if her love did not glorify and crown him. Ah! if I could but merge this terrible egotism which oppresses me, into the being of some one who is what I would wish to be were I man! I would not ask him to achieve fame. Enough if I felt that he was worthy of it, and happier methinks to console him when he failed than

to triumph with him when he won. Tell me, have
you felt this? When you loved did you stoop as to
a slave, or did you bow down as to a master?

From Madame de Grantmesnil to Isaura Cicogna.

Chère enfant,—All your four letters have reached
me the same day. In one of my sudden whims I set
off with a few friends on a rapid tour along the
Riviera to Genoa, thence to Turin on to Milan. Not
knowing where we should rest even for a day, my
letters were not forwarded.

I came back to Nice yesterday, consoled for all
fatigues in having insured that accuracy in description
of localities which my work necessitates.

You are, my poor child, in that revolutionary crisis
through which genius passes in youth before it knows
its own self, and longs vaguely to do or to be a something other than it has done or has been before. For,
not to be unjust to your own powers, genius you have
—that inborn undefinable essence, including talent,
and yet distinct from it. Genius you have, but genius
unconcentrated, undisciplined. I see, though you are
too diffident to say so openly, that you shrink from
the fame of singer, because, fevered by your reading,
you would fain aspire to the thorny crown of author.
I echo the hard saying of the *Maestro*, I should be
your worst enemy did I encourage you to forsake a
career in which a dazzling success is so assured, for
one in which, if it were your true vocation, you would
not ask whether you were fit for it; you would be

impelled to it by the terrible star which presides over the birth of poets.

Have you, who are so naturally observant, and of late have become so reflective, never remarked that authors, however absorbed in their own craft, do not wish their children to adopt it? The most successful author is perhaps the last person to whom neophytes should come for encouragement. This I think is not the case with the cultivators of the sister arts. The painter, the sculptor, the musician, seem disposed to invite disciples and welcome acolytes. As for those engaged in the practical affairs of life, fathers mostly wish their sons to be as they have been.

The politician, the lawyer, the merchant, each says to his children, "Follow my steps." All parents in practical life would at least agree in this—they would not wish their sons to be poets. There must be some sound cause in the world's philosophy for this general concurrence of digression from a road of which the travellers themselves say to those whom they love best, "Beware!"

Romance in youth is, if rightly understood, the happiest nutriment of wisdom in after-years; but I would never invite any one to look upon the romance of youth as a thing

"To case in periods and embalm in ink."

Enfant, have you need of a publisher to create romance? Is it not in yourself? Do not imagine that genius requires for its enjoyment the scratch of the

7*

pen and the types of the printer. Do not suppose
that the poet, the *romancier*, is most poetic, most romantic, when he is striving, struggling, labouring, to
check the rush of his ideas, and materialise the images
which visit him as souls into such tangible likenesses
of flesh and blood that the highest compliment a
reader can bestow on them is to say that they are life-
like? No: the poet's real delight is not in the
mechanism of composing; the best part of that delight
is in the sympathies he has established with innumerable modifications of life and form, and art and
nature—sympathies which are often found equally
keen in those who have not the same gift of language.
The poet is but the interpreter. What of?—Truths
in the hearts of others. He utters what they feel. Is the
joy in the utterance? Nay, it is in the feeling itself.
So, my dear, dark-bright child of song, when I bade
thee open, out of the beaten thoroughfare, paths into
the meads and river-banks at either side of the formal
hedgerows, rightly dost thou add that I enjoined thee
to make thine art thy companion. In the culture of
that art for which you are so eminently gifted, you will
find the ideal life ever beside the real. Are you not
ashamed to tell me that in that art you do but utter the
thoughts of others? You utter them in music; through the
music you not only give to the thoughts a new character, but you make them reproductive of fresh thoughts
in your audience.

You said very truly that you found in composing
you could put into music thoughts which you could

not put into words. That is the peculiar distinction of music. No genuine musician can explain
in words exactly what he means to convey in his
music.

How little a *libretto* interprets an opera—how little
we care even to read it! It is the music that speaks
to us; and how!—Through the human voice. We do
not notice how poor are the words which the voice
warbles. It is the voice itself interpreting the soul of
the musician which enchants and enthralls us. And
you who have that voice pretend to despise the gift.
What! despise the power of communicating delight!—
the power that we authors envy; and rarely, if ever,
can we give delight with so little alloy as the singer.

And when an audience disperses, can you guess
what griefs the singer may have comforted? what hard
hearts he may have softened? what high thoughts he
may have awakened?

You say, "Out on the vamped-up hypocrite! Out
on the stage-robes and painted cheeks!"

I say, "Out on the morbid spirit which so cynic-
ally regards the mere details by which a whole effect
on the minds and hearts and souls of races and nations
can be produced!"

There, have I scolded you sufficiently? I should
scold you more, if I did not see in the affluence of
your youth and your intellect the cause of your restlessness. Riches are always restless. It is only to
poverty that the gods give content.

You question me about love: you ask if I have

ever bowed to a master, ever merged my life in another's: expect no answer on this from me. Circe herself could give no answer to the simplest maid, who, never having loved, asks, "What is love?"

In the history of the passions each human heart is a world in itself; its experience profits no others. In no two lives does love play the same part or bequeath the same record.

I know not whether I am glad or sorry that the word "love" now falls on my ear with a sound as slight and as faint as the dropping of a leaf in autumn may fall on thine.

I volunteer but this lesson, the wisest I can give, if thou canst understand it: as I bade thee take art into thy life, so learn to look on life itself as an art. Thou couldst discover the charm in Tasso; thou couldst perceive that the requisite of all art, that which pleases, is in the harmony of proportion. We lose sight of beauty if we exaggerate the feature most beautiful.

Love proportioned, adorns the homeliest existence; love disproportioned, deforms the fairest.

Alas! wilt thou remember this warning when the time comes in which it may be needed?

E—— G——.

BOOK II.

CHAPTER L

It is several weeks after the date of the last chapter; the lime-trees in the Tuileries are clothed in green.

In a somewhat spacious apartment on the ground-floor in the quiet locality of the Rue d'Anjou, a man was seated, very still, and evidently absorbed in deep thought, before a writing-table placed close to the window.

Seen thus, there was an expression of great power both of intellect and of character in a face which, in ordinary social commune, might rather be notice-able for an aspect of hardy frankness, suiting well with the clear-cut, handsome profile, and the rich dark auburn hair, waving carelessly over one of those broad open foreheads, which, according to an old writer, seem the "frontispiece of a temple dedicated to Honour."

The forehead, indeed, was the man's most remark-able feature. It could not but prepossess the be-holder. When, in private theatricals, he had need to alter the character of his countenance, he did it effectually, merely by forcing down his hair till it reached his eyebrows. He no longer then looked like the same man.

The person I describe has been already intro-duced to the reader as Graham Vane. But perhaps

this is the fit occasion to enter into some such
details as to his parentage and position as may
make the introduction more satisfactory and complete.

His father, the representative of a very ancient
family, came into possession, after a long minority, of
what may be called a fair squire's estate, and about
half a million in moneyed investments, inherited on
the female side. Both land and money were absolutely
at his disposal, unencumbered by entail or settlement.
He was a man of a brilliant, irregular genius, of princely
generosity, of splendid taste, of a gorgeous kind of
pride closely allied to a masculine kind of vanity. As
soon as he was of age he began to build, converting
his squire's hall into a ducal palace. He then stood
for the county; and in days before the first Reform
Bill, when a county election was to the estate of a
candidate what a long war is to the debt of a nation.
He won the election; he obtained early successes in
Parliament. It was said by good authorities in political circles that, if he chose, he might aspire to lead
his party, and ultimately to hold the first rank in the
government of his country.

That may or may not be true; but certainly he did ·
not choose to take the trouble necessary for such an
ambition. He was too fond of pleasure, of luxury, of
pomp. He kept a famous stud of racers and hunters.
He was a munificent patron of art. His establishments,
his entertainments, were on a par with those of the
great noble who represented the loftiest (Mr. Vane

would not own it to be the eldest) branch of his
genealogical tree.

He became indifferent to political contests, indolent
in his attendance at the House, speaking seldom, not
at great length nor with much preparation, but with
power and fire, originality and genius; so that he was
not only effective as an orator, but combining with
eloquence advantages of birth, person, station, the
reputation of patriotic independence, and genial attributes of character, he was an authority of weight in
the scales of party.

This gentleman, at the age of forty, married the
dowerless daughter of a poor but distinguished naval
officer, of noble family, first cousin to the Duke of
Alton.

He settled on her a suitable jointure, but declined
to tie up any portion of his property for the benefit
of children by the marriage. He declared that so
much of his fortune was invested either in mines, the
produce of which was extremely fluctuating, or in
various funds, over rapid transfers in which it was
his amusement and his interest to have control, un-
checked by reference to trustees, that entails and
settlements on children were an inconvenience he declined to incur.

Besides, he held notions of his own as to the
wisdom of keeping children dependent on their father.
"What numbers of young men," said he, "are ruined
in character and in fortune by knowing that when
their father dies they are certain of the same provision,

no matter how they displease him; and in the meanwhile forestalling that provision by recourse to usurers."
These arguments might not have prevailed over the
bride's father a year or two later, when, by the death
of intervening kinsmen, he became Duke of Alton; but
in his then circumstances the marriage itself was so
much beyond the expectations which the portionless
daughter of a sea-captain has the right to form, that
Mr. Vane had it all his own way, and he remained
absolute master of his whole fortune, save of that part
of his landed estate on which his wife's jointure was
settled; and even from this encumbrance he was very
soon freed. His wife died in the second year of
marriage, leaving an only son—Graham. He grieved
for her loss with all the passion of an impressionable,
ardent, and powerful nature. Then for a while he
sought distraction to his sorrow by throwing himself
into public life with a devoted energy he had not previously displayed.

His speeches served to bring his party into power,
and he yielded, though reluctantly, to the unanimous
demand of that party that he should accept one of the
highest offices in the new Cabinet. He acquitted
himself well as an administrator, but declared, no
doubt honestly, that he felt like Sinbad released from
the old man on his back, when, a year or two afterwards, he went out of office with his party. No
persuasions could induce him to come in again; nor
did he ever again take a very active part in debate.
"No," said he, "I was born to the freedom of a private

gentleman—intolerable to me is the thraldom of a public servant. But I will bring up my son so that he may acquit the debt which I decline to pay to my country." There he kept his word. Graham had been carefully educated for public life, the ambition for it dinned into his ear from childhood. In his school-vacations his father made him learn and declaim chosen specimens of masculine oratory; engaged an eminent actor to give him lessons in elocution; bade him frequent theatres, and study there the effect which words derive from looks and gesture encouraged him to take part himself in private theatricals. To all this the boy lent his mind with delight. He had the orator's inborn temperament; quick, yet imaginative, and loving the sport of rivalry and contest. Being also, in his boyish years, good-humoured and joyous, he was not more a favourite with the masters in the school-room than with boys in the play-ground. Leaving Eton at seventeen, he then entered at Cambridge, and became, in his first term, the most popular speaker at the Union.

But his father cut short his academical career, and decided, for reasons of his own, to place him at once in Diplomacy. He was attached to the Embassy at Paris, and partook of the pleasures and dissipations of that metropolis too keenly to retain much of the sterner ambition to which he had before devoted himself. Becoming one of the spoiled darlings of fashion, there was great danger that his character would relax into the easy grace of the Epicurean,

when all such loiterings in the Rose Garden were
brought to abrupt close by a rude and terrible change
in his fortunes.

His father was killed by a fall from his horse in
hunting; and when his affairs were investigated, they
were found to be hopelessly involved—apparently the
assets would not suffice for the debts.   The elder
Vane himself was probably not aware of the extent of
his liabilities.   He had never wanted ready money to
the last. He could always obtain that from a money-
lender, or from the sale of his funded investments.
But it became obvious, on examining his papers, that
he knew at least how impaired would be the heritage
he should bequeath to a son whom he idolised.   For
that reason he had given Graham a profession in
diplomacy, and for that reason he had privately applied
to the Ministry for the Viceroyalty of India, in the
event of its speedy vacancy. He was eminent enough
not to anticipate refusal, and with economy in that
lucrative post much of his pecuniary difficulties might
have been redeemed, and at least an independent
provision secured for his son.

Graham, like Alain de Rochebriant, allowed no
reproach on his father's memory—indeed, with more
reason than Alain, for the elder Vane's fortune had at
least gone on no mean and frivolous dissipation.

It had lavished itself on encouragement to art—on
great objects of public beneficence—on public-spirited
aid of political objects; and even in mere selfish enjoyments there was a certain grandeur in his princely

hospitalities, in his munificent generosity, in a warm-hearted carelessness for money. No indulgence in petty follies or degrading vices aggravated the offence of the magnificent squanderer.

"Let me look on my loss of fortune as a gain to myself," said Graham, manfully. "Had I been a rich man, my experience of Paris tells me that I should most likely have been a very idle one. Now that I have no gold, I must dig in myself for iron."

The man to whom he said this was an uncle-in-law—if I may use that phrase—the Right Hon. Richard King, popularly styled "the blameless King."

This gentleman had married the sister of Graham's mother, whose loss in his infancy and boyhood she had tenderly and anxiously sought to supply. It is impossible to conceive a woman more fitted to invite love and reverence than was Lady Janet King, her manners were so sweet and gentle, her whole nature so elevated and pure.

Her father had succeeded to the dukedom when she married Mr. King, and the alliance was not deemed quite suitable. Still it was not one to which the Duke would have been fairly justified in refusing his assent.

Mr. King could not, indeed, boast of noble ances-try, nor was he even a landed proprietor; but he was a not undistinguished member of Parliament, of irre-proachable character, and ample fortune inherited from a distant kinsman, who had enriched himself as a merchant. It was on both sides a marriage of love.

It is popularly said that a man uplifts a wife to
his own rank; it as often happens that a woman uplifts her husband to the dignity of her own character.
Richard King rose greatly in public estimation after
his marriage with Lady Janet.

She united to a sincere piety a very active and a
very enlightened benevolence. She guided his ambition aside from mere party politics into subjects of
social and religious interest, and in devoting himself
to these he achieved a position more popular and
more respected than he could ever have won in the
strife of party.

When the Government of which the elder Vane
became a leading Minister was formed, it was considered a great object to secure a name so high in the
religious world, so beloved by the working classes, as
that of Richard King; and he accepted one of those
places which, though not in the Cabinet, confers the
rank of Privy Councillor.

When that brief-lived Administration ceased, he
felt the same sensation of relief that Vane had felt,
and came to the same resolution never again to accept office, but from different reasons, all of which
need not now be detailed. Amongst them, however,
certainly this: — He was exceedingly sensitive to
opinion, thin-skinned as to abuse, and very tenacious
of the respect due to his peculiar character of sanctity
and philanthropy. He writhed under every newspaper
article that had made "the blameless King" responsible for the iniquities of the Government to which he

belonged. In the loss of office he seemed to recover his former throne.

Mr. King heard Graham's resolution with a grave approving smile, and his interest in the young man became greatly increased. He devoted himself strenuously to the object of saving to Graham some wrecks of his paternal fortunes, and having a clear head and great experience in the transaction of business, he succeeded beyond the most sanguine expectations formed by the family solicitor. A rich manufacturer was found to purchase at a fancy price the bulk of the estate with the palatial mansion, which the estate alone could never have sufficed to maintain with suitable establishments.

So that when all debts were paid, Graham found himself in possession of a clear income of about £500 a-year, invested in a mortgage secured on a part of the hereditary lands, on which was seated an old hunting-lodge bought by a brewer.

With this portion of the property Graham parted very reluctantly. It was situated amid the most picturesque scenery on the estate, and the lodge itself was a remnant of the original residence of his ancestors before it had been abandoned for that which, built in the reign of Elizabeth, had been expanded into a Trentham-like palace by the last owner.

But Mr. King's argument reconciled him to the sacrifice. "I can manage," said the prudent adviser, "if you insist on it, to retain that remnant of the hereditary estate which you are so loath to part with. But how! by mortgaging it to an extent that will scarcely leave you £50 a-year net from the rents. This is not all. Your mind will then be distracted from the large object of a career to the small object of retaining a few family acres; you will be constantly hampered by private anxieties and fears: you could do nothing for the benefit of those around you—could not repair a farmhouse for a better class of tenant—could not rebuild a labourer's dilapidated cottage. Give up an idea that might be very well for a man whose sole ambition was to remain a squire, however beggarly. Launch yourself into the larger world of metropolitan life with energies wholly unshackled, a mind wholly undisturbed, and secure of an income which, however modest, is equal to that of most young men who enter that world as your equals."

Graham was convinced, and yielded, though with a bitter pang. It is hard for a man whose fathers have lived on the soil to give up all trace of their whereabouts. But none saw in him any morbid consciousness of change of fortune, when, a year after his father's death, he reassumed his place in society. If before courted for his expectations, he was still courted for himself; by many of the great who had loved his father, perhaps even courted more.

He resigned the diplomatic career, not merely because the rise in that profession is slow, and in the intermediate steps the chances of distinction are slight and few, but more because he desired to cast his lo in the home country, and regarded the courts of other lands as exile.

It was not true, however, as Lemercier had stated on report, that he lived on his pen. Curbing all his old extravagant tastes, £500 a-year amply supplied his wants. But he had by his pen gained distinction, and created great belief in his abilities for a public career. He had written critical articles, read with much praise, in periodicals of authority, and had published one or two essays on political questions, which had created yet more sensation. It was only the graver literature, connected more or less with his ultimate object of a public career, in which he had thus evinced his talents of composition. Such writings were not of a nature to bring him much money, but they gave him a definite and solid station. In the old time, before the first Reform Bill, his reputation would have secured him at once a seat in Parliament; but the ancient nurseries of statesmen are gone, and their place is not supplied.

He had been invited, however, to stand for more than one large and populous borough, with very fair prospects of success; and whatever the expense, Mr. King had offered to defray it. But Graham would not have incurred the latter obligation; and when he learned the pledges which his supporters would have exacted, he would not have stood if success had been certain and the cost nothing. "I cannot," he said to his friends, "go into the consideration of what is best for the country with my thoughts manacled; and I

cannot be both representative and slave of the greatest
ignorance of the greatest number. I bide my time,
and meanwhile I prefer to write as I please, rather
than vote as I don't please."

Three years went by, passed chiefly in England,
partly in travel; and at the age of thirty, Graham Vane
was still one of those of whom admirers say, "He will
be a great man some day;" and detractors reply, "Some
day seems a long way off."

The same fastidiousness which had operated against
that entrance into Parliament to which his ambition
not the less steadily adapted itself, had kept him free
from the perils of wedlock. In his heart he yearned
for love and domestic life, but he had hitherto met
with no one who realised the ideal he had formed.
With his person, his accomplishments, his connections,
and his repute, he might have made many an advantageous marriage. But somehow or other the charm
vanished from a fair face, if the shadow of a money-
bag fell on it; on the other hand, his ambition occupied so large a share in his thoughts that he would
have fled in time from the temptation of a marriage
that would have overweighted him beyond the chance
of rising. Added to all, he desired in a wife an intellect that, if not equal to his own, could become so
by sympathy — a union of high culture and noble
aspiration, and yet of loving womanly sweetness which
a man seldom finds out of books; and when he does
find it, perhaps it does not wear the sort of face that

he fancies. Be that as it may, Graham was still unmarried and heart-whole.

And now a new change in his life befell him.
Lady Janet died of a fever contracted in her habitual
rounds of charity among the houses of the poor. She
had been to him as the most tender mother, and a
lovelier soul than hers never alighted on the earth.
His grief was intense; but what was her husband's?—
one of those griefs that kill.

To the side of Richard King his Janet had been
as the guardian angel. His love for her was almost
worship—with her, every object in a life hitherto so
active and useful seemed gone. He evinced no noisy
passion of sorrow. He shut himself up, and refused
to see even Graham. But after some weeks had passed,
he admitted the clergyman in whom, on spiritual matters, he habitually confided, and seemed consoled by
the visits; then he sent for his lawyer, and made his
will; after which he allowed Graham to call on him
daily, on the condition that there should be no reference to his loss. He spoke to the young man on
other subjects, rather drawing him out about himself,
sounding his opinion on various grave matters, watch-
ing his face while he questioned, as if seeking to dive
into his heart, and sometimes pathetically sinking into
silence, broken but by sighs. So it went on for a few
more weeks; then he took the advice of his physician
to seek change of air and scene. He went away alone,
without even a servant, not leaving word where he
had gone. After a little while he returned, more ailing,

more broken than before. One morning he was found insensible—stricken by paralysis. He regained consciousness, and even for some days rallied strength. He might have recovered, but he seemed as if he tacitly refused to live. He expired at last, peacefully, in Graham's arms.

At the opening of his will it was found that he had left Graham his sole heir and executor. Deducting Government duties, legacies to servants, and donations to public charities, the sum thus bequeathed to his lost wife's nephew was two hundred and twenty thousand pounds.

With such a fortune, opening indeed was made for an ambition so long obstructed. But Graham affected no change in his mode of life; he still retained his modest bachelor's apartments—engaged no servants —bought no horses—in no way exceeded the income he had possessed before. He seemed, indeed, depressed rather than elated by the succession to a wealth which he had never anticipated.

Two children had been born from the marriage of Richard King; they had died young, it is true, but Lady Janet at the time of her own decease was not too advanced in years for the reasonable expectation of other offspring; and even after Richard King became a widower, he had given to Graham no hint of his testamentary dispositions. The young man was no blood-relation to him, and naturally supposed that such relations would become the heirs. But in truth the deceased seemed to have no blood-relations—none had ever been known to visit him—none raised a voice to question the justice of his will.

Lady Janet had been buried at Kensal Green; her husband's remains were placed in the same vault.

For days and days Graham went his way lonelily to the cemetery. He might be seen standing motionless by that tomb, with tears rolling down his cheeks; yet his was not a weak nature—not one of those that love indulgence of irremediable grief. On the contrary, people who did not know him well said "that he had more head than heart," and the character of his pursuits, as of his writings, was certainly not that of a sentimentalist. He had not thus visited the tomb till Richard King had been placed within it. Yet his love for his aunt was unspeakably greater than that which he could have felt for her husband. Was it, then, the husband that he so much more acutely mourned; or was there something that, since the husband's death, had deepened his reverence for the memory of her whom he had not only loved as a mother, but honoured as a saint?

These visits to the cemetery did not cease till Graham was confined to his bed by a very grave illness—the only one he had ever known. His physician said it was nervous fever, and occasioned by moral shock or excitement; it was attended with delirium. His recovery was slow, and when it was sufficiently completed he quitted England; and we find him now, with his mind composed, his strength restored, and his spirits braced, in that gay city of

Paris, hiding, perhaps, some earnest purpose amid his
participation in its holiday enjoyments.

He is now, as I have said, seated before his writing-
table in deep thought. He takes up a letter which he
had already glanced over hastily, and reperuses it with
more care.

The letter is from his cousin, the Duke of Alton,
who had succeeded a few years since to the family
honours—an able man, with no small degree of information, an ardent politician, but of very rational
and temperate opinions; too much occupied by the
cares of a princely estate to covet office for himself;
too sincere a patriot not to desire office for those to
whose hands he thought the country might be most
safely intrusted—an intimate friend of Graham's.
The contents of the letter are these:—

MY DEAR GRAHAM,—I trust that you will welcome
the brilliant opening into public life which these lines
are intended to announce to you. Vavasour has just
been with me to say that he intends to resign his seat
for the county when Parliament meets, and agreeing
with me that there is no one so fit to succeed him as
yourself, he suggests the keeping his intention secret
until you have arranged your committee and are pre-
pared to take the field. You cannot hope to escape
a contest; but I have examined the Register, and the
party has gained rather than lost since the last election,
when Vavasour was so triumphantly returned. The
expenses for this county, where there are so many

out-voters to bring up, and so many agents to retain,
are always large in comparison with some other coun-
ties; but that consideration is all in your favour, for
it deters Squire Hunston, the only man who could
beat you, from starting; and to your resources a thousand pounds more or less are a trifle not worth dis-
cussing. You know how difficult it is nowadays to
find a seat for a man of moderate opinions like yours
and mine. Our county would exactly suit you. The
constituency is so evenly divided between the urban
and rural populations, that its representative must
fairly consult the interests of both. He can be neither
an ultra-Tory nor a violent Radical. He is left to
the enviable freedom, to which you say you aspire, of
considering what is best for the country as a whole.

Do not lose so rare an opportunity. There is but
one drawback to your triumphant candidature. It will
be said that you have no longer an acre in the county
in which the Vanes have been settled so long. That
drawback can be removed. It is true that you can
never hope to buy back the estates which you were
compelled to sell at your father's death—the old
manufacturer gripes them too firmly to loosen his
hold; and after all, even were your income double
what it is, you would be overhoused in the vast pile
in which your father buried so large a share of his
fortune. But that beautiful old hunting-lodge, the
Stamm Schloss of your family, with the adjacent farms,
can be now repurchased very reasonably. The brewer
who bought them is afflicted with an extravagant son,

whom he placed in the——Hussars, and will gladly
sell the property for £5000 more than. he gave: well
worth the difference, as he has improved the farm-
buildings and raised the rental. I think, in addition
to the sum you have on mortgage, £23,000 will be
accepted, and as a mere investment pay you nearly
three per cent. But to you it is worth more than
double the money; it once more identifies your ancient
name with the county. You would be a greater personage with that moderate holding in the district in
which your race took root, and on which your father's
genius threw such a lustre, than you would be if you
invested all your wealth in a county in which every
squire and farmer would call you "the new man."
Pray think over this most seriously, and instruct your
solicitor to open negotiations with the brewer at once.
But rather put yourself into the train, and come back
to England straight to me. I will ask Vavasour to
meet you. What news from Paris? Is the Emperor as
ill as the papers insinuate? And is the revolutionary
party gaining ground?—Your affectionate cousin,

                                        ALTON.

As he put down this letter, Graham heaved a short
impatient sigh.

"The old *Stamm Schloss*," he muttered—"a foot
on the old soil once more! and an entrance into the
great arena with hands unfettered. Is it possible!—
is it—is it?"

At this moment the door-bell of the apartment rang,

and a servant whom Graham had hired at Paris as a *laquais de place* announced "*Ce Monsieur.*"

Graham hurried the letter into his portfolio, and said, "You mean the person to whom I am always at home?"

"The same, Monsieur."

"Admit him, of course."

There entered a wonderfully thin man, middle-aged, clothed in black, his face cleanly shaven, his hair cut very short, with one of those faces which, to use a French expression, say "nothing." It was absolutely without expression—it had not even, despite its thinness, one salient feature. If you had found yourself anywhere seated next to that man, your eye would have passed him over as too insignificant to notice; if at a *café*, you would have gone on talking to your friend without lowering your voice. What mattered it whether a *bête* like that overheard or not? Had you been asked to guess his calling and station, you might have said, minutely observing the freshness of his clothes and the undeniable respectability of his *tout ensemble*, "He must be well off, and with no care for customers on his mind—a *ci-devant* chandler who has retired on a legacy."

Graham rose at the entrance of his visitor, motioned him courteously to a seat beside him, and waiting till the *laquais* had vanished, then asked "What news?"

"None, I fear, that will satisfy Monsieur. I have certainly hunted out, since I had last the honour to

see you, no less than four ladies of the name of Duval,
but only one of them took that name from her parents,
and was also christened Louise."

"Ah— Louise!"

"Yes, the daughter of a perfumer, aged twenty-eight.
She, therefore, is not the Louise you seek. Permit me
to refer to your instructions." Here M. Renard took
out a note-book, turned over the leaves, and resumed
—"Wanted, Louise Duval, daughter of Auguste Duval,
a French drawing-master, who lived for many years at
Tours, removed to Paris in 1845, lived at No. 12 Rue
de S—— at Paris for some years, but afterwards moved
to a different *quartier* of the town, and died, 1848, in
Rue L——, No. 39. Shortly after his death, his
daughter Louise left that lodging, and could not be
traced. In 1849 official documents reporting her death
were forwarded from Munich to a person (a friend of
yours, Monsieur). Death, of course, taken for granted;
but nearly five years afterwards, this very person encountered the said Louise Duval at Aix-la-Chapelle,
and never heard nor saw more of her. *Demande* submitted, to find out said Louise Duval or any children
of hers born in 1848-9; supposed in 1852-3 to have
one child, a girl, between four and five years old. Is
that right, Monsieur?"

"Quite right."

"And this is the whole information given to me.
Monsieur on giving it asked me if I thought it desirable
that he should commence inquiries at Aix-la-Chapelle,
where Louise Duval was last seen by the person in-

terested to discover her. I reply, No; — pains thrown
away. Aix-la-Chapelle is not a place where any Frenchwoman not settled there by marriage would remain.
Nor does it seem probable that the said Duval would
venture to select for her residence Munich, a city in
which she had contrived to obtain certificates of her
death. A Frenchwoman who has once known Paris
always wants to get back to it, especially, Monsieur, if
she has the beauty which you assign to this lady. I
therefore suggested that our inquiries should commence
in this capital. Monsieur agreed with me, and I did
not grudge the time necessary for investigation."

"You were most obliging. Still I am beginning to
be impatient if time is to be thrown away."

"Naturally. Permit me to return to my notes.
Monsieur informs me that twenty-one years ago, in
1848, the Parisian police were instructed to find out
this lady and failed, but gave hopes of discovering her
through her relations. He asks me to refer to our
archives; I tell him that is no use. However, in order
to oblige him, I do so. No trace of such inquiry—it
must have been, as Monsieur led me to suppose, a
strictly private one, unconnected with crime or with
politics; and as I have the honour to tell Monsieur, no
record of such investigations is preserved in our office.
Great scandal would there be, and injury to the peace
of families, if we preserved the results of private inquiries intrusted to us—by absurdly jealous husbands,
for instance. Honour, Monsieur, honour forbids it.
Next I suggest to Monsieur that his simplest plan would

be an advertisement in the French journals, stating, if I understand him right, that it is for the pecuniary interest of Madame or Mademoiselle Duval, daughter of Auguste Duval, *artiste en dessin*, to come forward. Monsieur objects to that."

"I object to it extremely; as I have told you, this is a strictly confidential inquiry, and an advertisement, which in all likelihood would be practically useless (it proved to be so in a former inquiry), would not be resorted to unless all else failed, and even then with reluctance."

"Quite so. Accordingly, Monsieur delegates to me, who have been recommended to him as the best person he can employ in that department of our police which is not connected with crime or political *surveillance*, a task the most difficult. I have, through strictly private investigations, to discover the address and prove the identity of a lady bearing a name among the most common in France, and of whom nothing has been heard for fifteen years, and then at so migratory an *endroit* as Aix-la-Chapelle. You will not or cannot inform me if since that time the lady has changed her name by marriage."

"I have no reason to think that she has; and there are reasons against the supposition that she married after 1849."

"Permit me to observe that the more details of information Monsieur can give me, the easier my task of research will be."

"I have given you all the details I can, and, aware

of the difficulty of tracing a person with a name so much the reverse of singular, I adopted your advice in our first interview, of asking some Parisian friend of mine, with a large acquaintance in the miscellaneous societies of your capital, to inform me of any ladies of that name whom he might chance to encounter; and he, like you, has lighted upon one or two, who, alas! resemble the right one in name, and nothing more."

"You will do wisely to keep him on the watch as well as myself. If it were but a murderess or a political·incendiary, then you might trust exclusively to the enlightenment of our *corps*, but this seems an affair of sentiment, Monsieur. Sentiment is not in our way. Seek the trace of that in the haunts of pleasure."

M. Renard, having thus poetically delivered himself of that philosophical dogma, rose to depart.

Graham slipped into his hand a bank-note of sufficient value to justify the profound bow he received in return.

When M. Renard had gone, Graham heaved another impatient sigh, and said to himself, "No, it is not possible—at least not yet."

Then, compressing his lips as a man who forces himself to something he dislikes, he dipped his pen into the inkstand, and wrote rapidly thus to his kinsman:—

MY DEAR COUSIN,—I lose not a post in replying to your kind and considerate letter. It is not in my power at present to return to England. I need not say how fondly I cherish the hope of representing the dear old county some day. If Vavasour could be induced to defer his resignation of the seat for another session, or at least for six or seven months, why then I might be free to avail myself of the opening; at present I am not. Meanwhile I am sorely tempted to buy back the old Lodge—probably the brewer would allow me to leave on mortgage the sum I myself have on the property, and a few additional thousands. I have reasons for not wishing to transfer at present much of the money now invested in the funds. I will consider this point, which probably does not press.

I reserve all Paris news till my next; and begging you to forgive so curt and unsatisfactory a reply to a letter so important that it excites me more than I like to own, believe me, your affectionate friend and cousin,

GRAHAM.

CHAPTER IL

At about the same hour on the same day in which
the Englishman held the conference with the Parisian
detective just related, the Marquis de Rochebriant found
himself by appointment in the *cabinet d'affaires* of his
avoué M. Gandrin: that gentleman had hitherto not
found time to give him a definitive opinion as to the
case submitted to his judgment. The *avoué* received
Alain with a kind of forced civility, in which the natural intelligence of the Marquis, despite his inexperience of life, discovered embarrassment.

"Monsieur le Marquis," said Gandrin, fidgeting
among the papers on his bureau, "this is a very com-
plicated business. I have given not only my best attention to it, but to your general interests. To be plain,
your estate, though a fine one, is fearfully encumbered
—fearfully—frightfully."

"Sir," said the Marquis, haughtily, "that is a fact
which was never disguised from you."

"I do not say that it was, Marquis; but I scarcely
realised the amount of the liabilities nor the nature of
the property. It will be difficult—nay, I fear, impossible
—to find any capitalist to advance a sum that will
cover the mortgages at an interest less than you now
pay. As for a Company to take the whole trouble off

your hands, clear off the mortgages, manage the forests,
develop the fisheries, guarantee you an adequate income, and at the end of twenty-one years or so render
up to you or your heirs the free enjoyment of an estate
thus improved, we must dismiss that prospect as a
wild dream of my good friend M. Hébert's. People
in the provinces do dream; in Paris everybody is wide
awake."

"Monsieur," said the Marquis, with that inborn
imperturbable loftiness of *sang froid* which has always
in adverse circumstances characterised the French
noblesse, "be kind enough to restore my papers. I
see that you are not the man for me. Allow me only
to thank you, and inquire the amount of my debt for
the trouble I have given."

"Perhaps you are quite justified in thinking I am
not the man for you, Monsieur le Marquis; and your
papers shall, if you decide on dismissing me, be returned to you this evening. But as to my accepting
remuneration where I have rendered no service, I request M. le Marquis, to put that out of the question.
Considering myself, then, no longer your *avoué*, do
not think I take too great a liberty in volunteering my
counsel as a friend—or a friend at least to M. Hébert,
if you do not vouchsafe my right so to address yourself."

M. Gandrin spoke with a certain dignity of voice
and manner which touched and softened his listener.

"You make me your debtor far more than I pretend to repay," replied Alain. "Heaven knows I want

a friend, and I will heed with gratitude and respect all your counsels in that character."

"Plainly and briefly, my advice is this: Monsieur Louvier is the principal mortgagee. He is among the six richest capitalists of Paris. He does not, therefore, want money, but, like most self-made men, he is very accessible to social vanities. He would be proud to think he had rendered a service to a Rochebriant. Approach him, either through me, or, far better, at once introduce yourself, and propose to consolidate all your other liabilities in one mortgage to him, at a rate of interest lower than that which is now paid to some of the small mortgagees. This would add considerably to your income and would carry out M. Hébert's advice."

"But does it not strike you, dear M. Gandrin, that such going cap-in-hand to one who has power over my fate, while I have none over his, would scarcely be consistent with my self-respect, not as Rochebriant only, but as Frenchman?"

"It does not strike me so in the least; at all events, I could make the proposal on your behalf, without compromising yourself, though I should be far more sanguine of success if you addressed M. Louvier in person."

"I should nevertheless prefer leaving it in your hands; but even for that I must take a few days to consider. Of all the mortgagees M. Louvier has been hitherto the severest and most menacing, the one whom Hébert dreads the most; and should he become

9*

sole mortgagee, my whole estate would pass to him if, through any succession of bad seasons and failing tenants, the interest was not punctually paid."

"It could so pass to him now."

"No; for there have been years in which the other mortgagees, who are Bretons, and would be loath to ruin a Rochebriant, have been lenient and patient."

"If Louvier has not been equally so, it is only because he knew nothing of you, and your father no doubt had often sorely tasked his endurance. Come, suppose we manage to break the ice easily. Do me the honour to dine here to meet him; you will find that he is not an unpleasant man."

The Marquis hesitated, but the thought of the sharp and seemingly hopeless struggle for the retention of his ancestral home to which he would be doomed if he returned from Paris unsuccessful in his errand overmastered his pride. He felt as if that self-conquest was a duty he owed to the very tombs of his fathers. "I ought not to shrink from the face of a creditor," said he, smiling somewhat sadly, "and I accept the proposal you so graciously make."

"You do well, Marquis, and I will write at once to Louvier to ask him to give me his first disengaged day."

The Marquis had no sooner quitted the house than M. Gandrin opened a door at the side of his office, and a large portly man strode into the room —stride it was rather than step—firm, self-assured, arrogant, masterful.

"Well, *mon ami*," said this man, taking his stand at the hearth, as a king might take his stand in the hall of his vassal—"and what says our *petit muscadin?*"

"He is neither *petit* nor *muscadin*, Monsieur Louvier," replied Gandrin, peevishly; "and he will task your powers to get him thoroughly into your net. But I have persuaded him to meet you here. What day can you dine with me? I had better ask no one else."

"To-morrow I dine with my friend O——, to meet the chiefs of the Opposition," said Mons. Louvier, with a sort of careless rollicking pomposity. "Thursday with Pereire—Saturday I entertain at home. Say Friday. Your hour?"

"Seven."

"Good! Show me those Rochebriant papers again; there is something I had forgotten to note. Never mind me. Go on with your work as if I were not here."

Louvier took up the papers, seated himself in an arm-chair by the fireplace, stretched out his legs, and read at his ease, but with a very rapid eye, as a practised lawyer skims through the technical forms of a case to fasten upon the marrow of it.

"Ah! as I thought. The farms could not pay even the interest on my present mortgage; the forests come in for that. If a contractor for the yearly sale of the woods was bankrupt and did not pay, how could I get my interest? Answer me that, Gandrin."

"Certainly you must run the risk of that chance."

"Of course the chance occurs, and then I foreclose*—I, seize,—Rochebriant and its *seigneuries* are mine."

As he spoke he laughed, not sardonically,—a jovial laugh—and opened wide, to reshut as in a vice, the strong iron hand, which had doubtless closed over many a man's all.

"Thanks. On Friday, seven o'clock." He tossed the papers back on the bureau, nodded a royal nod, and strode forth imperiously as he had strided in.

* For the sake of the general reader, English technical words are here, as elsewhere, substituted as much as possible for French.

CHAPTER IIL

MEANWHILE the young Marquis pursued his way
thoughtfully through the streets, and entered the
Champs Elysées. Since we first, nay, since we last
saw him, he is strikingly improved in outward ap-
pearances. He has unconsciously acquired more of
the easy grace of the Parisian in gait and bearing.
You would no longer detect the Provincial—perhaps,
however, because he is now dressed, though very
simply, in habiliments that belong to the style of the
day. Rarely among the loungers in the Champs
Elysées could be seen a finer form, a comelier face,
an air of more unmistakable distinction.

The eyes of many a passing fair one gazed on
him, admiringly or coquettishly. But he was still so
little the true Parisian that they got no smile, no look
in return. He was wrapt in his own thoughts; was he
thinking of M. Louvier?

He had nearly gained the entrance of the Bois de
Boulogne, when he was accosted by a voice behind,
and turning round saw his friend Lemercier arm-in-
arm with Graham Vane.

"*Bonjour*, Alain," said Lemercier, hooking his
disengaged arm into Rochebriant's. "I suspect we
are going the same way."

Alain felt himself change countenance at this con-
jecture, and replied coldly, "I think not; I have got
to the end of my walk, and shall turn back to Paris;"
addressing himself to the Englishman, he said with
formal politeness, "I regret not to have found you at
home when I called some weeks ago, and no less so
to have been out when you had the complaisance to
return my visit."

"At all events," replied the Englishman, "let me
not lose the opportunity of improving our acquaintance which now offers.   It is true that our friend
Lemercier, catching sight of me in the Rue de Rivoli,
stopped his *coupé* and carried me off for a promenade
in the Bois. The fineness of the day tempted us to
get out of his carriage as the Bois came in sight. But
if you are going back to Paris I relinquish the Bois
and offer myself as your companion."

Frederic (the name is so familiarly English that
the reader might think me pedantic did I accentuate
it as French) looked from one to the other of his two
friends, half amused and half angry.

"And am I to be left alone to achieve a conquest,
in which, if I succeed, I shall change into hate and
envy the affection of my two best friends?—Be it so.

'Un véritable amant ne connaît point d'amis.' "

"I do not comprehend your meaning," said the
Marquis, with a compressed lip and a slight frown.

"Bah!" cried Frederic; "come, *franc jeu*—cards
on the table—M. Gram Varn was going into the Bois

at my suggestion on the chance of having another look at the pearl-coloured angel; and you, Rochebriant, can't deny that you were going into the Bois for the same object."

"One may pardon an *enfant terrible*," said the Englishman, laughing, "but an *ami terrible* should be sent to the galleys. Come, Marquis, let us walk back and submit to our fate. Even were the lady once more visible, we have no chance of being observed by the side of a Lovelace so accomplished and so audacious!"

"Adieu, then, recreants—I go alone. Victory or death."

The Parisian beckoned his coachman, entered his carriage, and with a mocking grimace kissed his hand to the companions thus deserting or deserted.

Rochebriant touched the Englishman's arm, and said, "Do you think that Lemercier could be impertinent enough to accost that lady?"

"In the first place," returned the Englishman, "Lemercier himself tells me that the lady has for several weeks relinquished her walks in the Bois, and the probability is, therefore, that he will not have the opportunity to accost her. In the next place, it appears that when she did take her solitary walk, she did not stray far from her carriage, and was in reach of the protection of her *laquais* and coachman. But to speak honestly, do you who know Lemercier better than I, take him to be a man who would commit an imper-

tinence to a woman unless there were *viveurs* of his
own sex to see him do it?"

Alain smiled. "No. Frederic's real nature is an
admirable one, and if he ever do anything that he
ought to be ashamed of, 'twill be from the pride of
showing how finely he can do it. Such was his character at college, and such it still seems at Paris. But
it is true that the lady has forsaken her former walk;
at least I—I have not seen her since the day I first
beheld her in company with Frederic. Yet—yet, pardon me, you were going to the Bois on the chance
of seeing her. Perhaps she has changed the direction
of her walk, and—and——."

The Marquis stopped short, stammering and confused.

The Englishman scanned his countenance with
the rapid glance of a practised observer of men and
things, and after a short pause, said: "If the lady
has selected some other spot for her promenade, I
am ignorant of it; nor have I even volunteered the
chance of meeting with her, since I learned—first
from Lemercier, and afterwards from others—that her
destination is the stage. Let us talk frankly, Marquis.
I am accustomed to take much exercise on foot, and
the Bois is my favourite resort: one day I there
found myself in the *allée* which the lady we speak of
used to select for her promenade, and there saw her.
Something in her face impressed me; how shall I
describe the impression? Did you ever open a poem,
a romance, in some style, wholly new to you, and

before you were quite certain whether or not its merits
justified the interest which the novelty inspired, you
were summoned away, or the book was taken out of
your hands? If so, did you not feel an intellectual
longing to have another glimpse of the book? That
illustration describes my impression, and I own that I
twice again went to the same *allée*. The last time I
only caught sight of the young lady as she was getting into her carriage. As she was then borne away,
I perceived one of the custodians of the Bois; and
learned, on questioning him, that the lady was in
the habit of walking always alone in the same *allée*
at the same hour on most fine days, but that he did
not know her name or address. A motive of curiosity
—perhaps an idle one—then made me ask Lemercier,
who boasts of knowing his Paris so intimately, if he
could inform me who the lady was. He undertook to
ascertain."

"But," interposed the Marquis, "he did not ascertain who she was; he only ascertained where she
lived, and that she and an elder companion were
Italians,—whom he suspected, without sufficient ground,
to be professional singers."

"True; but since then I ascertained more detailed
particulars from two acquaintances of mine who happen
to know her—M. Savarin, the distinguished writer,
and Mrs. Morley, an accomplished and beautiful
American lady, who is more than an acquaintance.
I may boast the honour of ranking among her friends.
As Savarin's villa is at A——, I asked him inciden-

tally if he knew the fair neighbour whose face had so attracted me; and Mrs. Morley being present, and overhearing me, I learned from both what I now repeat to you.

"The young lady is a Signorina Cicogna—at Paris exchanging (except among particular friends), as is not unusual, the outlandish designation of Signorina for the more conventional one of Mademoiselle. Her father was a member of the noble Milanese family of the same name, therefore the young lady is well born. Her father has been long dead; his widow married again an English gentleman settled in Italy, a scholar and antiquarian; his name was Selby. This gentleman, also dead, bequeathed the Signorina a small but sufficient competence. She is now an orphan, and residing with a companion, a Signora Venosta, who was once a singer of some repute at the Neapolitan Theatre, in the orchestra of which her husband was principal performer; but she relinquished the stage several years ago on becoming a widow, and gave lessons as a teacher. She has the character of being a scientific musician, and of unblemished private respectability. Subsequently she was induced to give up general teaching, and undertake the musical education and the social charge of the young lady with her. This girl is said to have early given promise of extraordinary excellence as a singer, and excited great interest among a coterie of literary critics and musical *cognoscenti*. She was to have come out at the Theatre of Milan a year or two ago, but her

career has been suspended in consequence of ill-
health, for which she is now at Paris under the care
of an English physician, who has made remarkable
cures in all complaints of the respiratory organs.
M * * *, the great composer, who knows her, says that
in expression and feeling she has no living superior,
perhaps no equal since Malibran."

"You seem, dear Monsieur, to have taken much
pains to acquire this information."

"No great pains were necessary; but had they
been I might have taken them, for, as I have owned
to you, Mademoiselle Cicogna, while she was yet a
mystery to me, strangely interested my thoughts or
my fancies. That interest has now ceased. The world
of actresses and singers lies apart from mine."

"Yet," said Alain, in a tone of voice that implied
doubt, "if I understand Lemercier aright, you were
going with him to the Bois on the chance of seeing
again the lady in whom your interest has ceased."

"Lemercier's account was not strictly accurate.
He stopped his carriage to speak to me on quite
another subject, on which I have consulted him, and
then proposed to take me on to the Bois. I assented;
and it was not till we were in the carriage that he
suggested the idea of seeing whether the pearly-robed
lady had resumed her walk in the *allée*. You may
judge how indifferent I was to that chance when I
preferred turning back with you to going on with
him. Between you and me, Marquis, to men of our
age, who have the business of life before them, and

feel that if there be aught in which *noblesse oblige* it
is a severe devotion to noble objects, there is nothing
more fatal to such devotion than allowing the heart
to be blown hither and thither at every breeze of
mere fancy, and dreaming ourselves into love with
some fair creature whom we never could marry con-
sistently with the career we have set before our ambition. I could not marry an actress—neither, I presume,
could the Marquis de Rochebriant; and the thought.
of a courtship, which excluded the idea of marriage,
to a young orphan of name unblemished—of virtue
unsuspected—would certainly not be compatible with
'devotion to noble objects.'"

Alain involuntarily bowed his head in assent to
the proposition, and, it may be, in submission to an
implied rebuke.   The two men walked in silence for
some minutes, and Graham first spoke, changing
altogether the subject of conversation.

"Lemercier tells me you decline going much into
this world of Paris—the capital of capitals—which
appears so irresistibly attractive to us foreigners."

"Possibly; but, to borrow your words, I have the
business of life before me."

"Business is a good safeguard against the temp-
tations to excess in pleasure, in which Paris abounds.
But there is no business which does not admit of
some holiday, and all business necessitates commerce
with mankind. *A propos*, I was the other evening at
the Duchesse de Tarascon's—a brilliant assembly,

filled with ministers, senators, and courtiers. I heard your name mentioned."

"Mine?"

"Yes; Duplessis, the rising financier—who rather to my surprise was not only present among these official and decorated celebrities, but apparently quite at home among them—asked the Duchess if she had not seen you since your arrival at Paris. She replied, 'No; that though you were among her nearest connections, you had not called on her;' and bade Duplessis tell you that you were a *monstre* for not doing so. Whether or not Duplessis will take that liberty I know not; but you must pardon me if I do. She is a very charming woman, full of talent; and that stream of the world which reflects the stars, with all their mythical influences on fortune, flows through her *salons*."

"I am not born under those stars. I am a Legitimist."

"I did not forget your political creed; but in England the leaders of opposition attend the *salons* of the Prime Minister. A man is not supposed to compromise his opinions because he exchanges social courtesies with those to whom his opinions are hostile. Pray excuse me if I am indiscreet;—I speak as a traveller who asks for information—but do the Legitimists really believe that they best serve their cause by declining any mode of competing with its opponents? Would there not be a fairer chance for the ultimate victory of their principles if they made their talents and energies individually prominent—if they were

known as skilful generals, practical statesmen, eminent
diplomatists, brilliant writers?—could they combine—
not to sulk and exclude themselves from the great
battle-field of the world—but in their several ways to
render themselves of such use to their country that
some day or other, in one of those revolutionary
crises to which France, alas! must long be subjected,
they would find themselves able to turn the scale of
undecided councils and conflicting jealousies?"

"Monsieur, we hope for the day when the Divine
Disposer of events will strike into the hearts of our
fickle and erring countrymen the conviction that there
will be no settled repose for France save under the
sceptre of her rightful kings. But meanwhile we are
—I see it more clearly since I have quitted Bretagne
—we are a hopeless minority."

"Does not history tell us that the great changes of
the world have been wrought by minorities? but on
the one condition that the minorities shall not be
hopeless? It is almost the other day that the Bona-
partists were in a minority that their adversaries called
hopeless, and the majority for the Emperor is now so
preponderant that I tremble for his safety. When a
majority becomes so vast that intellect disappears in
the crowd, the date of its destruction commences; for
by the law of reaction the minority is installed against
it. It is the nature of things that minorities are always
more intellectual than multitudes, and intellect is ever
at work in sapping numerical force. What your party
want is hope; because without hope there is no
energy. I remember hearing my father say that when

he met the Count de Chambord at Ems, that illustrious personage delivered himself of a *belle phrase* much admired by his partisans. The Emperor was then President of the Republic, in a very doubtful and dangerous position. France seemed on the verge of another convulsion. A certain distinguished politician recommended the Count de Chambord to hold himself ready to enter at once as a candidate for the throne. And the Count, with a benignant smile on his handsome face, answered, 'All wrecks come to the shore—the shore does not go to the wrecks.'"

"Beautifully said!" exclaimed the Marquis.

"Not if *Le beau est toujours le vrai.* My father, no inexperienced nor unwise politician, in repeating the royal words, remarked: 'The fallacy of the Count's argument is in its metaphor. A man is not a shore. Do you not think that the seamen on board the wrecks would be more grateful to him who did not complacently compare himself to a shore, but considered himself a human being like themselves, and risked his own life in a boat, even though it were a cockle-shell, in the chance of saving theirs?'"

Alain de Rochebriant was a brave man, with that intense sentiment of patriotism which characterises Frenchmen of every rank and persuasion, unless they belong to the Internationalists; and without pausing to consider, he cried, "Your father was right."

The Englishman resumed: "Need I say, my dear Marquis, that I am not a Legitimist? I am not an Imperialist, neither am I an Orleanist nor a Republican.

Between all those political divisions it is for Frenchmen to make their choice, and for Englishmen to accept for France that government which France has established. I view things here as a simple observer. But it strikes me that if I were a Frenchman in your position, I should think myself unworthy my ancestors if I consented to be an insignificant looker-on."

"You are not in my position," said the Marquis, half mournfully, half haughtily, "and you can scarcely judge of it even in imagination."

"I need not much task my imagination; I judge of it by analogy. I was very much in your position when I entered upon what I venture to call my career; and it is the curious similarity between us in circumstances that made me wish for your friendship when that similarity was made known to me by Lemercier, who is not less garrulous than the true Parisian usually is. Permit me to say that, like you, I was reared in some pride of no inglorious ancestry. I was reared also in the expectation of great wealth. Those expectations were not realised: my father had the fault of noble natures—generosity pushed to imprudence: he died poor and in debt. You retain the home of your ancestors; I had to resign mine."

The Marquis had felt deeply interested in this narrative, and as Graham now paused, took his hand and pressed it.

"One of our most eminent personages said to me about that time, 'Whatever a clever man of your age determines to do or to be, the odds are twenty to one that he has only to live on in order to do or to be it.' Don't you think he spoke truly? I think so."

"I scarcely know what to think," said Rochebriant; "I feel as if you had given me so rough a shake when I was in the midst of a dull dream, that I am not yet quite sure whether I am asleep or awake."

Just as he said this, and towards the Paris end of the Champs Elysées, there was a halt, a sensation among the loungers round them: many of them uncovered in salute.

A man on the younger side of middle age, somewhat inclined to corpulence, with a very striking countenance, was riding slowly by. He returned the salutations he received with the careless dignity of a Personage accustomed to respect, and then reined in his horse by the side of a barouche, and exchanged some words with a portly gentleman who was its sole occupant. The loungers, still halting, seemed to contemplate this parley—between him on horseback and him in the carriage—with very eager interest. Some put their hands behind their ears and pressed forward, as if trying to overhear what was said.

"I wonder," quoth Graham, "whether, with all his cleverness, the Prince has in any way decided what *he* means to do or to be."

"The Prince!" said Rochebriant, rousing himself from reverie; "what Prince?"

"Do you not recognise him by his wonderful likeness to the first Napoleon—him on horseback talking to Louvier, the great financier."

10*

"Is that stout *bourgeois* in the carriage Louvier—
my mortgagee, Louvier?"

"Your mortgagee, my dear Marquis? Well, he is
rich enough to be a very lenient one upon pay-day."

"*Hein!*—I doubt his leniency," said Alain. "I have
promised my *avoué* to meet him at dinner. Do you
think I did wrong?"

"Wrong! of course not; he is likely to overwhelm
you with civilities. Pray don't refuse if he gives you
an invitation to his *soirée* next Saturday—I am going
to it. One meets there the notabilities most interesting to study—artists, authors, politicians, especially
those who call themselves Republicans. He and the
Prince agree in one thing—viz., the cordial reception
they give to the men who would destroy the state
of things upon which Prince and financier both thrive.
Hillo! here .comes Lemercier on return from the Bois."

Lemercier's *coupé* stopped beside the footpath. "What
tidings of the *Belle Inconnue?*" asked the Englishman.

"None; she was not there. But I am rewarded—
such an adventure—a dame of the *haute volée*—I believe she is a duchess. She was walking with a lap-
dog, a pure Pomeranian. A strange poodle flew at
the Pomeranian. I drove off the poodle, rescued
the Pomeranian, received the most gracious thanks,
the sweetest smile:—*femme superbe*, middle-aged. I
prefer women of forty. *Au revoir*, I am due at the club."

Alain felt a sensation of relief that Lemercier had
not seen the lady in the pearl-coloured dress, and
quitted the Englishman with a lightened heart.

CHAPTER IV.

"Piccola, piccola! com' è cortese! another invitation from M. Louvier for next Saturday— *conversazione."* This was said in Italian by an elderly lady bursting noisily into the room—elderly, yet with a youthful expression of face, owing perhaps to a pair of very vivacious black eyes. She was dressed, after a somewhat slatternly fashion, in a wrapper of crimson merino much the worse for wear, a blue handkerchief twisted turban-like round her head, and her feet encased in list slippers. The person to whom she addressed herself was a young lady with dark hair, which, despite its evident redundance, was restrained into smooth glossy braids over the forehead, and at the crown of the small graceful head into the simple knot which Horace has described as "Spartan." Her dress contrasted the speaker's by as exquisite neatness. We have seen her before as the lady in the pearl-coloured robe, but seen now at home she looks much younger. She was one of those whom, encountered in the streets or in society, one might guess to be married—probably a young bride; for thus seen there was about her an air of dignity and of self-possession which suits well with the ideal of chaste youthful matronage; and in the expression of the face there was a pensive thought-

fulness beyond her years. But as she now sat by the
open window arranging flowers in a glass bowl, a
book lying open on her lap, you would never have
said, "What a handsome woman!" you would have
said, "What a charming girl!" All about her was
maidenly, innocent, and fresh. The dignity of her
bearing was lost in household ease, the pensiveness
of her expression in an untroubled serene sweetness.

Perhaps many of my readers may have known
friends engaged in some absorbing cause of thought,
and who are in the habit when they go out, especially if on solitary walks, to take that cause of thought
with them. The friend may be an orator meditating
his speech, a poet his verses, a lawyer a difficult case,
a physician an intricate malady. If you have such a
friend, and you observe him thus away from his home,
his face will seem to you older and graver. He is
absorbed in the care that weighs on him. When you
see him in a holiday moment at his own fireside, the
care is thrown aside; perhaps he mastered while
abroad the difficulty that had troubled him; he is
cheerful, pleasant, sunny. This appears to be very
much the case with persons of genius. When in their
own houses we usually find them very playful and
childlike. Most persons of real genius, whatever they
may seem out of doors, are very sweet-tempered at
home, and sweet temper is sympathising and genial in
the intercourse of private life. Certainly, observing
this girl as she now bends over the flowers; it would
be difficult to believe her to be the Isaura Cicogna

whose letters to Madame de Grantmesnil exhibit the doubts and struggles of an unquiet, discontented, aspiring mind. Only in one or two passages in those letters would you have guessed at the writer in the girl as we now see her.

It is in those passages where she expresses her love of harmony, and her repugnance to contest— those were characteristics you might have read in her face.

Certainly the girl is very lovely: what long dark eyelashes—what soft, tender, dark-blue eyes! now that she looks up and smiles, what a bewitching smile it is! — by what sudden play of rippling dimples the smile is enlivened and redoubled! Do you notice one feature? in very showy beauties it is seldom noticed; but I, being in my way a physiognomist, consider that it is always worth heeding as an index of character. It is the ear. Remark how delicately it is formed in her—none of that heaviness of lobe which is a sure sign of sluggish intellect and coarse perception. Hers is the artist's ear. Note next those hands—how beautifully shaped! small, but not doll-like hands—ready and nimble, firm and nervous hands, that could work for a helpmate. By no means very white, still less red, but somewhat embrowned as by the sun, such as you may see in girls reared in southern climates, and in her perhaps betokening an impulsive character which had not accustomed itself, when at sport in the open air, to the thraldom of gloves—very impulsive people even in cold climates seldom do.

In conveying to us by a few bold strokes an idea of the sensitive, quick-moved, warm-blooded Henry II., the most impulsive of the Plantagenets, his contemporary chronicler tells us that rather than imprison those active hands of his, even in hawking-gloves, he would suffer his falcon to fix its sharp claws into his wrist. No doubt there is a difference as to what is befitting between a burly bellicose creature like Henry II. and a delicate young lady like Isaura Cicogna; and one would not wish to see those dainty wrists of hers seamed and scarred by a falcon's claws. But a girl may not be less exquisitely feminine for slight heed of artificial prettinesses. Isaura had no need of pale bloodless hands to seem one of Nature's highest grade of gentlewomen even to the most fastidious eyes. About her there was a charm apart from her mere beauty, and often disturbed instead of heightened by her mere intellect: it consisted in a combination of exquisite artistic refinement, and of a generosity of character by which refinement was animated into vigour and warmth.

The room, which was devoted exclusively to Isaura, had in it much that spoke of the occupant. That room, when first taken furnished, had a good deal of the comfortless showiness which belongs to ordinary furnished apartments in France, especially in the Parisian suburbs, chiefly let for the summer—thin limp muslin curtains that decline to draw, stiff mahogany chairs covered with yellow Utrecht velvet, a tall *secrétaire* in a dark corner, an oval buhl-table set in tawdry ormolu, islanded in the centre of a poor but gaudy Scotch carpet, and but one other table of dull walnut-wood standing clothless before a sofa to match the chairs; the eternal ormolu clock flanked by the two eternal ormolu candelabra on the dreary mantelpiece. Some of this garniture had been removed, others softened into cheeriness and comfort. The room somehow or other,—thanks partly to a very moderate expenditure in pretty twills with pretty borders, gracefully simple table-covers, with one or two additional small tables and easy-chairs, two simple vases filled with flowers—thanks still more to a nameless skill in rearrangement, and the disposal of the slight nick-nacks and well-bound volumes, which, even in travelling, women who have cultivated the pleasures of taste carry about with them,—had been coaxed into that quiet harmony, that tone of consistent subdued colour, which corresponded with the characteristics of the inmate. Most people might have been puzzled where to place the piano, a semi-grand, so as not to take up too much space in the little room; but where it was placed it seemed so at home that you might have supposed the room had been built for it.

There are two kinds of neatness—one is too evident, and makes everything about it seem trite and cold and stiff, and another kind of neatness disappears from our sight in a satisfied sense of completeness— like some exquisite, simple, finished style of writing— an Addison's or a St. Pierre's.

This last sort of neatness belonged to Isaura, and
brought to mind the well-known line of Catullus when
on recrossing his threshold he invokes its welcome
—a line thus not inelegantly translated by Leigh
Hunt—

"Smile every dimple on the cheek of Home."

I entreat the reader's pardon for this long descriptive
digression; but Isaura is one of those characters which
are called many-sided, and therefore not very easy to
comprehend. She gives us one side of her character
in her correspondence with Madame de Grantmesnil,
and another side of it in her own home with her
Italian companion—half nurse, half *chaperon*.

"Monsieur Louvier is indeed very courteous,"
said Isaura, looking up from the flowers with the
dimpled smile we have noticed. "But I think, *Madre*,
that we should do well to stay at home on Saturday
—not peacefully, for I owe you your revenge at
Euchre."

"You can't mean it, *Piccola!*" exclaimed the
Signora in evident consternation. "Stay at home!—
why stay at home! *Euchre* is very well when there is
nothing else to do; but change is pleasant—*le bon
Dieu* likes it—

' Ne caldo ne gelo
Resta mai in cielo.'

And such beautiful ices one gets at M. Louvier's. Did
you taste the Pistachio ice? What fine rooms, and so
well lit up!—I adore light. And the ladies so beauti-

fully dressed—one sees the fashions. Stay at home—
play at *Euchre* indeed! *Piccola*, you cannot be so
cruel to yourself—you are young."

"But, dear *Madre*, just consider—we are invited
because we are considered professional singers: your
reputation as such is of course established—mine is
not; but still I shall be asked to sing as I was asked
before; and you know Dr. C—— forbids me to do so
except to a very small audience; and it is so ungraci-
ous always to say 'No;' and besides, did you not yourself say, when we came away last time from M. Louvier's, that it was very dull—that you knew nobody
—and that the ladies had such superb toilets that you
felt mortified—and——"

"*Zitto! zitto!* you talk idly, *Piccola*—very idly. I
was mortified then in my old black Lyons silk; but
have I not bought since then my beautiful Greek
jacket—scarlet and gold lace? and why should I buy
it if I am not to show it?"

"But, dear *Madre*, the jacket is certainly very
handsome, and will make an effect in a little dinner at
the Savarins or Mrs. Morley's. But in a great formal
reception like M. Louvier's will it not look——"

"Splendid!" interrupted the Signora.

"But *singolare*."

"So much the better; did not that great English
lady wear such a jacket, and did not every one admire her—*più tosto invidia che compassione?*"

Isaura sighed. Now the jacket of the Signora was
a subject of disquietude to her friend. It so happened

that a young English lady of the highest rank and the rarest beauty had appeared at M. Louvier's, and indeed generally in the *beau monde* of Paris, in a Greek jacket that became her very much. That jacket had fascinated, at M. Louvier's the eyes of the Signora. But of this Isaura was unaware. The Signora, on returning home from M. Louvier's, had certainly lamented much over the *mesquin* appearance of her old-fashioned Italian habiliments compared with the brilliant toilet of the gay Parisiennes; and Isaura — quite woman enough to sympathise with woman in such womanly vanities—proposed the next day to go with the Signora to one of the principal *couturières* of Paris, and adapt the Signora's costume to the fashions of the place. But the Signora having predetermined on a Greek jacket, and knowing by instinct that Isaura would be disposed to thwart that splendid predilection, had artfully suggested that it would be better to go to the *couturière* with Madame Savarin, as being a more experienced adviser,—and the *coupé* only held two.

As Madame Savarin was about the same age as the Signora, and dressed as became her years, and in excellent taste, Isaura thought this an admirable suggestion; and pressing into her *chaperon's* hand a *billet de banque* sufficient to re-equip her *cap-à-pie*, dismissed the subject from her mind. But the Signora was much too cunning to submit her passion for the Greek jacket to the discouraging comments of Madame Savarin. Monopolising the *coupé*, she became absolute mistress of the situation. She went to no fashionable *couturière's.* She went to a *magasin* that she had seen advertised in the *Petites Affiches* as supplying superb costumes for fancy-balls and amateur performers in private theatricals. She returned home triumphant, with a jacket still more 'dazzling to the eye than that of the English lady.

When Isaura first beheld it, she drew back in a sort of superstitious terror, as of a comet or other blazing portent.

"*Cosa stupenda!*"—(stupendous thing!) She might well be dismayed when the Signora proposed to appear thus attired in M. Louvier's *salon.* What might be admired as coquetry of dress in a young beauty of rank so great that even a vulgarity in her would be called *distinguée*, was certainly an audacious challenge of ridicule in the elderly *ci-devant* music-teacher.

But how could Isaura, how can any one of common humanity, say to a woman resolved upon wearing a certain dress, "You are not young and handsome enough for that"?—Isaura could only murmur, "For many reasons I would rather stay at home, dear *Madre.*"

"Ah! I see you are ashamed of me," said the Signora, in softened tones: "very natural. When the nightingale sings no more, she is only an ugly brown bird:" and therewith the Signora Venosta seated herself submissively, and began to cry.

On this Isaura sprang up, wound her arms round the Signora's neck, soothed her with coaxing, kissed and petted her, and ended by saying, "Of course we

will go;" and, "but let me choose you another dress
—a dark-green velvet trimmed with blonde—blonde
becomes you so well."

"No, no—I hate green velvet; anybody can wear
that. *Piccola*, I am not clever like thee; I cannot
amuse myself like thee with books. I am in a foreign
land. I have a poor head, but I have a big heart"
(another burst of tears); "and that big heart is set on
my beautiful Greek jacket."

"Dearest *Madre*," said Isaura, half weeping too,
"forgive me; you are right. The Greek jacket is
splendid; I shall be so pleased to see you wear it.
Poor *Madre*—so pleased to think that in the foreign
land you are not without something that pleases
you."

CHAPTER V.

CONFORMABLY with his engagement to meet M. Louvier, Alain found himself on the day and at the hour named in M. Gandrin's *salon*. On this occasion Madame Gandrin did not appear. Her husband was accustomed to give *diners d'hommes*. The great man had not yet arrived. "I think, Marquis," said M. Gandrin, "that you will not regret having followed my advice: my representations have disposed Louvier to regard you with much favour, and he is certainly flattered by being permitted to make your personal acquaintance."

The *avoué* had scarcely finished this little speech, when M. Louvier was announced. He entered with a beaming smile, which did not detract from his imposing presence. His flatterers had told him that he had a look of Louis Philippe; therefore he had sought to imitate the dress and the *bonhomie* of that monarch of the middle class. He wore a wig, elaborately piled up, and shaped his whiskers in royal harmony with the royal wig. Above all, he studied that social frankness of manner with which the able sovereign dispelled awe of his presence or dread of his astuteness. Decidedly he was a man very pleasant to converse and to deal with—so long as there seemed to him

something to gain and nothing to lose by being pleasant. He returned Alain's bow by a cordial offer of
both expansive hands, into the grasp of which the
hands of the aristocrat utterly disappeared. "Charmed
to make your acquaintance, Marquis — still more
charmed if you will let me be useful during your *séjour*
at Paris. *Ma foi*, excuse my bluntness, but you are a
fort beau garçon. Monsieur your father was a handsome man, but you beat him hollow. Gandrin, my
friend, would not you and I give half our fortunes for
one year of this fine fellow's youth spent at Paris!
Peste! what love-letters we should have, with no need
to buy them by *billets de banque!*" Thus he ran on,
much to Alain's confusion, till dinner was announced.
Then there was something *grandiose* in the frank
bourgeois style wherewith he expanded his napkin and
twisted one end into his waistcoat—it was so manly a
renunciation of the fashions which a man so *répandu*
in all circles might be supposed to follow;—as if he
were both too great and too much in earnest for such
frivolities. He was evidently a sincere *bon vivant*, and
M. Gandrin had no less evidently taken all requisite
pains to gratify his taste. The Montrachet served with
the oysters was of precious vintage. That *vin de
madère* which accompanied the *potage à la bisque*
would have contented an American. And how radiant
became Louvier's face, when amongst the *entrées* he
came upon *laitances de carpes!* "The best thing in the
world," he cried, "and one gets it so seldom since the
old Rocher de Cancale has lost its renown., At private

houses, what does one get now?—*blanc de poulet*—
flavourless trash. After all, Gandrin, when we lose
the love-letters, it is some consolation that *laitances de
carpes* and *sautés de foie gras* are still left to fill up the
void in our hearts. Marquis, heed my counsel; cultivate betimes the taste for the table; that and whist
are the sole resources of declining years. You never
met my old friend Talleyrand—ah, no! he was long
before your time. He cultivated both, but he made
two mistakes. No man's intellect is perfect on all
sides. He confined himself to one meal a-day, and
he never learned to play well at whist. Avoid his
errors, my young friend—avoid them. Gandrin, I
guess this pine-apple is English—it is superb."

"You are right—a present from the Marquis of
H——."

"Ah! instead of a fee, I wager. The Marquis
gives nothing for nothing, dear man! Droll people the
English. You have never visited England, I presume,
cher Rochebriant?"

The affable financier had already made vast progress in familiarity with his silent fellow-guest.

When the dinner was over and the three men had
re-entered the *salon* for coffee and liqueurs, Gandrin
left Louvier and Alain alone, saying he was going to
his cabinet for cigars which he could recommend.
Then Louvier, lightly patting the Marquis on the
shoulder, said with what the French call *effusion*,—
"My dear Rochebriant, your father and I did not
quite understand each other. He took a tone of

grand seigneur that sometimes wounded me; and I in turn was perhaps too rude in asserting my rights—as creditor, shall I say?—no, as fellow-citizen; and Frenchmen are so vain, so over-susceptible—fire up at a word—take offence when none is meant. We two, my dear boy, should be superior to such national foibles. *Bref*—I have a mortgage on your lands. Why should that thought mar our friendship? At my age, though I am not yet old, one is flattered if the young like us—pleased if we can oblige them, and remove from their career any little obstacle in its way. Gandrin tells me you wish to consolidate all the charges on your estate into one on a lower rate of interest. Is it so?"

"I am so advised," said the Marquis.

"And very rightly advised; come and talk with me about it some day next week. I hope to have a large sum of money set free in a few days. Of course, mortgages on land don't pay like speculations at the Bourse; but I am rich enough to please myself. We will see—we will see."

Here Gandrin returned with the cigars; but Alain at that time never smoked, and Louvier excused himself, with a laugh and a sly wink, on the plea that he was going to pay his respects—as doubtless that *joli garçon* was going to do, likewise—to a *belle dame* who did not reckon the smell of tobacco among the perfumes of Houbigant or Arabia.

"Meanwhile," added Louvier, turning to Gandrin, "I have something to say to you on business about

the contract for that new street of mine. No hurry
—after our young friend has gone to his 'assigna-
tion.'"

Alain could not misinterpret the hint; and in a
few moments took leave of his host more surprised
than disappointed that the financier had not invited
him, as Graham had assumed he would, to his *soirée*
the following evening.

When Alain was gone, Louvier's jovial manner
disappeared also, and became bluffly rude rather than
bluntly cordial.

"Gandrin, what did you mean by saying that that
young man was no *muscadin! Muscadin—aristocrate*
—offensive from top to toe."

"You amaze me—you seemed to take to him so
cordially."

"And pray, were you too blind to remark with
what cold reserve he responded to my condescen-
sions! How he winced when I called him Rochebriant! how he coloured when I called him 'dear
boy!' These aristocrats think we ought to thank them
on our knees when they take our money, and"—here
Louvier's face darkened—"seduce our women."

"Monsieur Louvier, in all France I do not know
a greater aristocrat than yourself."

I don't know whether M. Gandrin meant that
speech as a compliment, but M. Louvier took it as
such—laughed complacently and rubbed his hands.
"Ay, ay, *millionnaires* are the real aristocrats, for they
have power, as my *beau Marquis* will soon find. I

11*

must bid you good-night. Of course I shall see Madame Gandrin and yourself to-morrow. Prepare for a
motley gathering—lots of democrats and foreigners,
with artists and authors, and such creatures."

"Is that the reason why you did not invite the
Marquis?"

"'To be sure; I would not shock so pure a Legitimist by contact with the sons of the people, and
make him still colder to myself. No; when he comes
to my house he shall meet lions and *viveurs* of the
haut ton, who will play into my hands by teaching
him how to ruin himself in the quickest manner and
in the *genre Régence. Bon soir, mon vieux.*"

CHAPTER VI.

THE next night Graham in vain looked round for Alain in M. Louvier's *salons*, and missed his highbred mien and melancholy countenance. M. Louvier had been for some four years a childless widower, but his receptions were not the less numerously attended, nor his establishment less magnificently *monté* for the absence of a presiding lady: very much the contrary; it was noticeable how much he had increased his status and prestige as a social personage since the death of his unlamented spouse.

To say truth, she had been rather a heavy drag on his triumphal car. She had been the heiress of a man who had amassed a great deal of money; not in the higher walks of commerce, but in a retail trade.

Louvier himself was the son of a rich money-lender; he had entered life with an ample fortune and an intense desire to be admitted into those more brilliant circles in which fortune can be dissipated with *éclat*. He might not have attained this object but for the friendly countenance of a young noble who was then

"The glass of fashion and the mould of form."

But this young noble, of whom later we shall hear

more, came suddenly to grief; and when the money-
lender's son lost that potent protector, the dandies,
previously so civil, showed him a very cold shoulder.

Louvier then became an ardent democrat, and re-
cruited the fortune he had impaired by the aforesaid
marriage, launched into colossal speculations, and became enormously rich. His aspirations for social rank
now revived, but his wife sadly interfered with them.
She was thrifty by nature; sympathised little with her
husband's genius for accumulation; always said he
would end in a hospital; hated Republicans; despised
authors and artists; and by the ladies of the *beau
monde* was pronounced common and vulgar.

So long as she lived, it was impossible for Louvier
to realise his ambition of having one of the *salons*
which at Paris establish celebrity and position. He
could not then command those advantages of wealth
which he especially coveted. He was eminently successful in doing this now. As soon as she was safe
in Père la Chaise, he enlarged his hotel by the purchase and annexation of an adjoining house; re-
decorated and refurnished it, and in this task displayed,
it must be said to his credit, or to that of the admi-
nistrators he selected for the purpose, a nobleness of
taste rarely exhibited nowadays. His collection of
pictures was not large, and consisted exclusively of
the French school, ancient and modern, for in all
things Louvier affected the patriot. But each of those
pictures was a gem; such Watteaus, such Greuzes,
such landscapes by Patel, and, above all, such master-

pieces by Ingrès, Horace Vernet, and Delaroche, were worth all the doubtful originals of Flemish and Italian art which make the ordinary boast of private collectors.

These pictures occupied two rooms of moderate size, built for their reception, and lighted from above. The great *salon* to which they led contained treasures scarcely less precious; the walls were covered with the richest silks which the looms of Lyons could produce. Every piece of furniture here was a work of art in its way: console-tables of Florentine mosaic, inlaid with pearl and lapis-lazuli; cabinets in which the exquisite designs of the *renaissance* were carved in ebony; colossal vases of Russian malachite, but wrought by French artists. The very nick-nacks scattered carelessly about the room might have been admired in the cabinets of the Palazzo Pitti. Beyond this room lay the *salle de danse*, its ceiling painted by * * *, supported by white marble columns, the glazed balcony and the angles of the room filled with tiers of exotics. In the dining-room, on the same floor, on the other side of the landing-place, were stored in glazed buffets, not only vessels and salvers of plate, silver and gold, but, more costly still, matchless specimens of Sèvres and Limoges, and mediæval varieties of Venetian glass. On the ground-floor, which opened on the lawn of a large garden, Louvier had his suite of private apartments, furnished, as he said, "simply, according to English notions of comfort." Englishmen would have said "according to French notions

of luxury." Enough of these details, which a writer
cannot give without feeling himself somewhat vul-
garised in doing so, but without a loose general idea
of which a reader would not have an accurate con-
ception of something not vulgar—of something grave,
historical, possibly tragical, the existence of a Parisian
millionnaire at the date of this narrative.

The evidence of wealth was everywhere manifest
at M. Louvier's, but it was everywhere refined by an
equal evidence of taste. The apartments devoted to
hospitality ministered to the delighted study of artists,
to whom free access was given, and of whom two or
three might be seen daily in the "show-rooms," copy-
ing pictures or taking sketches of rare articles of furniture or effects for palatian interiors.

Among the things which rich English visitors of
Paris most coveted to see was M. Louvier's hotel; and
few among the richest left it without a sigh of envy
and despair. Only in such London houses as belong to a Sutherland or a Holford could our metropolis exhibit a splendour as opulent and a taste as
refined.

M. Louvier had his set evenings for popular as-
semblies. At these were entertained the Liberals of
every shade, from *tricolor* to *rouge*, with the artists
and writers most in vogue, *pêle-mêle* with decorated
diplomatists, ex-ministers, Orleanists, and Republicans,
distinguished foreigners, plutocrats of the Bourse, and
lions male and female from the arid nurse of that

race, the Chaussée d'Antin. Of his more select re-
unions something will be said later.

"And how does this poor Paris metamorphosed
please Monsieur Vane?" asked a Frenchman with a
handsome intelligent countenance, very carefully
dressed, though in a somewhat bygone fashion, and
carrying off his tenth lustrum with an air too sprightly
to evince any sense of the weight.

This gentleman, the Vicomte de Brézé, was of
good birth, and had a legitimate right to his title of
Vicomte, which is more than can be said of many
vicomtes one meets at Paris. He had no other property, however, than a principal share in an influential
journal, to which he was a lively and sparkling con-
tributor. In his youth, under the reign of Louis
Philippe, he had been a chief among literary exqui-
sites, and Balzac was said to have taken him more
than once as his model for those brilliant young *vau-
riens* who figure in the great novelist's comedy of
"Human Life." The Vicomte's fashion expired with
the Orleanist dynasty.

"Is it possible, my dear Vicomte," answered Graham, "not to be pleased with a capital so marvellously
embellished?"

"Embellished it may be to foreign eyes," said the
Vicomte, sighing, "but not improved to the taste of a
Parisian like me. I miss the dear Paris of old—the
streets associated with my *beaux jours* are no more.
Is there not something drearily monotonous in those
interminable perspectives? How frightfully the way

lengthens before one's eyes! In the twists and curves
of the old Paris one was relieved from the pain of
seeing how far one had to go from one spot to
another—each tortuous street had a separate idiosyn-
crasy; what picturesque diversities, what interesting
recollections—all swept away! *Mon Dieu!* and what
for? Miles of florid *façades* staring and glaring at
one with goggle-eyed pitiless windows. House-rents
trebled; and the consciousness that, if you venture to
grumble, underground railways, like concealed vol-
canoes, can burst forth on you at any moment with
an eruption of bayonets and muskets. This *maudit
empire* seeks to keep its hold on France much as a
grand seigneur seeks to enchain a nymph of the
ballet, tricks her out in finery and baubles, and in-
sures her infidelity the moment he fails to satisfy her
whims.

"Vicomte," answered Graham, "I have had the
honour to know you since I was a small boy at a
preparatory school home for the holidays, and you
were a guest at my father's country-house. You were
then *fêté* as one of the most promising writers among
the young men of the day, especially favoured by the
princes of the reigning family. I shall never forget
the impression made on me by your brilliant appearance and your no less brilliant talk."

"*Ah! ces beaux jours! ce bon Louis Philippe, ce
cher petit Joinville,*" sighed the Vicomte.

"But at that day you compared *le bon* Louis
Philippe to Robert Macaire. You described all his

sons, including, no doubt, *ce cher petit Joinville*, in terms of resentful contempt, as so many plausible *gamins* whom Robert Macaire was training to cheat the public in the interest of the family firm. I remember my father saying to you in answer, 'No royal house in Europe has more sought to develop the literature of an epoch, and to signalise its representatives by social respect and official honours, than that of the Orleans dynasty; you, M. de Brézé, do but imitate your elders in seeking to destroy the dynasty under which you flourish; should you succeed, you *hommes de plume* will be the first sufferers and the loudest complainers.' "

"*Cher Monsieur Vane*," said the Vicomte, smiling complacently, "your father did me great honour in classing me with Victor Hugo, Alexandre Dumas, Emile de Girardin, and the other stars of the Orleanist galaxy, including our friend here, M. Savarin. A very superior man was your father."

"And," said Savarin, who, being an Orleanist, had listened to Graham's speech with an approving smile —"and if I remember right, my dear De Brézé, no one was more brilliantly severe than yourself on poor De Lamartine and the Republic that succeeded Louis Philippe; no one more emphatically expressed the yearning desire for another Napoleon to restore order at home and renown abroad. Now you have got another Napoleon."

"And I want change for my Napoleon," said De Brézé, laughing.

"My dear Vicomte," said Graham, "one thing we may all grant, that in culture and intellect you are far superior to the mass of your fellow-Parisians; that you are therefore a favourable type of their political character."

"*Ah, mon cher, vous êtes trop aimable.*"

"And therefore I venture to say this, if the archangel Gabriel were permitted to descend to Paris and form the best government for France that the wisdom of seraph could devise, it would not be two years—I doubt if it would be six months—before out of this Paris, which you call the *Foyer des Idées*, would emerge a powerful party, adorned by yourself and other *hommes de plume*, in favour of a revolution for the benefit of *ce bon* Satan and *ce cher petit* Beelzebub."

"What a pretty vein of satire you have, *mon cher!*" said the Vicomte, good-humouredly; "there is a sting of truth in your witticism. Indeed, I must send you some articles of mine in which I have said much the same thing—*les beaux esprits se rencontrent.* The fault of us French is impatience—desire of change; but then it is that desire which keeps the world going and retains our place at the head of it. However, at this time we are all living too fast for our money to keep up with it, and too slow for our intellect not to flag. We vie with each other on the road to ruin, for in literature all the old paths to fame are shut up."

Here a tall gentleman, with whom the Vicomte had been conversing before he accosted Vane, and who had remained beside De Brézé listening in silent attention to this colloquy, interposed, speaking in the slow voice of one accustomed to measure his words, and with a slight but unmistakable German accent— "There is that, M. de Brézé, which makes one think gravely of what you say so lightly. Viewing things with the unprejudiced eyes of a foreigner, I recognise much for which France should be grateful to the Emperor. Under his sway her material resources have been marvellously augmented; her commerce has been placed by the treaty with England on sounder foundations, and is daily exhibiting richer life; her agriculture has made a prodigious advance wherever it has allowed room for capitalists, and escaped from the curse of petty allotments and peasant-proprietors—a curse which would have ruined any country less blessed by Nature; turbulent factions have been quelled; internal order maintained; the external prestige of France, up at least to the date of the Mexican war, increased to an extent that might satisfy even a Frenchman's *amour propre;* and her advance in civilisation has been manifested by the rapid creation of a naval power which should put even England on her mettle. But, on the other hand——"

"Ay, on the other hand," said the Vicomte.

"On the other hand there are in the imperial system two causes of decay and of rot silently at work. They may not be the faults of the Emperor, but they are such misfortunes as may cause the fall of the Empire. The first is an absolute divorce between the

political system and the intellectual culture of the
nation. The throne and the system rest on universal
suffrage—on a suffrage which gives to classes the most
ignorant a power that preponderates over all the
healthful elements of knowledge. It is the tendency
of all ignorant multitudes to personify themselves, as
it were, in one individual. They cannot comprehend
you when you argue for a principle; they do comprehend you when you talk of a name. The Emperor
Napoleon is to them a name, and the prefects and
officials who influence their votes are paid for incor-
porating all principles in the shibboleth of that single
name. You have thus sought the wellspring of a
political system in the deepest stratum of popular
ignorance. To rid popular ignorance of its normal
revolutionary bias, the rural peasants are indoctrinated
with the conservatism that comes from the fear which
appertains to property. They have their roods of land
or their shares in a national loan. Thus you estrange
the crassitude of an ignorant democracy still more
from the intelligence of the educated classes by combining it with the most selfish and abject of all the
apprehensions that are ascribed to aristocracy and
wealth. What is thus embedded in the depths of your
society makes itself shown on the surface. Napoleon III.
has been compared to Augustus; and there are many
startling similitudes between them in character and in
fate. Each succeeds to the heritage of a great name
that had contrived to unite autocracy with the popular
cause. Each subdued all rival competitors, and in-

augurated despotic rule in the name of freedom. Each mingled enough of sternness with ambitious will to stain with bloodshed the commencement of his power; but it would be an absurd injustice to fix the same degree of condemnation on the *coup d'état* as humanity fixes on the earlier cruelties of Augustus. Each, once firm in his seat, became mild and clement: Augustus perhaps from policy, Napoleon III. from a native kindliness of disposition which no fair critic of character can fail to acknowledge. Enough of similitudes; now for one salient difference. Observe how earnestly Augustus strove, and how completely he succeeded in the task, to rally round him all the leading intellects in every grade and of every party—the followers of Antony, the friends of Brutus—every great captain, every great statesman, every great writer, every man who could lend a ray of mind to his own Julian constellation, and make the age of Augustus an era in the annals of human intellect and genius. But this has not been the good fortune of your Emperor. The result of his system has been the suppression of intellect in every department. He has rallied round him not one great statesman; his praises are hymned by not one great poet. The *célébrités* of a former day stand aloof; or, preferring exile to constrained allegiance, assail him with unremitting missiles from their asylum in foreign shores. His reign is sterile of new *célébrités*. The few that arise enlist themselves against him. Whenever he shall venture to give full freedom to the press and to the legislature, the in-

tellect thus suppressed . or thus hostile will burst forth
in collected volume. His partisans have not been
trained and disciplined to meet such assailants. They
will be as weak as no doubt they will be violent. And
the worst is, that the intellect thus rising in mass
against him will be warped and distorted, like cap-
tives who, being kept in chains, exercise their limbs,
on escaping, in vehement jumps without definite
object. The directors of emancipated opinion may
thus be terrible enemies to the Imperial Government,
but they will be very unsafe councillors to France.
Concurrently with this divorce between the Imperial
system and the national intellect—a divorce so complete that even your *salons* have lost their wit, and
even your caricatures their point—a corruption of
manners which the Empire, I own, did not originate,
but inherit, has become so common that every one
owns and nobody blames it. The gorgeous ostenta-
tion of the Court has perverted the habits of the
people. The intelligence obstructed from other vents
betakes itself to speculating for a fortune; and the
greed of gain and the passion for show are sapping
the noblest elements of the old French manhood.
Public opinion stamps with no opprobrium a minister
or favourite who profits by a job; and I fear you
will find that jobbing pervades all your administrative
departments."

"All very true," said De Brézé, with a shrug of
the shoulders and in a tone of levity that seemed to
ridicule the assertion he volunteered; "Virtue and

Honour banished from courts and *salons* and the cabinets of authors, ascend to fairer heights in the attics of *ouvriers.*"

"The *ouvriers, ouvriers* of Paris!" cried this terrible German.

"Ay, Monsieur le Comte, what can you say against our *ouvriers?* A German count cannot condescend to learn anything about *ces petites gens.*"

"Monsieur," replied the German, "in the eyes of a statesman there are no *petites gens,* and in those of a philosopher no *petites choses.* We in Germany have too many difficult problems affecting our working classes to solve, not to have induced me to glean all the information I can as to the *ouvriers* of Paris. They have among them men of aspirations as noble as can animate the souls of philosophers and poets, perhaps not the less noble because common-sense and experience cannot follow their flight. But, as a body, the *ouvriers* of Paris have not been elevated in political morality by the benevolent aim of the Emperor to find them ample work and good wages independent of the natural laws that regulate the markets of labour. Accustomed thus to consider the State bound to maintain them, the moment the State fails in that impossible task, they will accommodate their honesty to a rush upon property under the name of social reform. Have you not noticed how largely increased within the last few years is the number of those who cry out, '*La Propriété, c'est le vol?*' Have you considered the rapid growth of the International Association? I do not say that for all these evils the Empire is exclusively responsible. To a certain degree they are found in all rich communities, especially where democracy is more or less in the ascendant. To a certain extent they exist in the large towns of Germany; they are conspicuously increasing in England; they are acknowledged to be dangerous in the United States of America; they are, I am told on good authority, making themselves visible with the spread of civilisation in Russia. But under the French Empire they have become glaringly rampant, and I venture to predict that the day is not far off when the rot at work throughout all layers and strata of French society will insure a fall of the fabric at the sound of which the world will ring.

"There is many a fair and stately tree which continues to throw out its leaves and rear its crest till suddenly the wind smites it, and then, and not till then, the trunk which seems so solid is found to be but the rind to a mass of crumbled powder."

"Monsieur le Comte," said the Vicomte, "you are a severe critic and a lugubrious prophet. But a German is so safe from revolution that he takes alarm at the stir of movement which is the normal state of the French *esprit.*"

"French *esprit* may soon evaporate into Parisian *bêtise.* As to Germany being safe from revolution, allow me to repeat a saying of Goethe's—but has M. le Vicomte ever heard of Goethe?"

"Goethe, of course—*très joli écrivain.*"

"Goethe said to some one who was making much the same remark as yourself, 'We Germans are in a state of revolution now, but we do things so slowly that it will be a hundred years before we Germans shall find it out. But when completed, it will be the greatest revolution society has yet seen, and will last like the other revolutions that, beginning, scarce noticed, in Germany, have transformed the world.'"

"*Diable*, M. le Comte! Germans transformed the world! What revolutions do you speak of?"

"The invention of gunpowder, the invention of printing, and the expansion of a monk's quarrel with his Pope into the Lutheran revolution."

Here the German paused, and asked the Vicomte to introduce him to Vane, which De Brézé did by the title of Count von Rudesheim. On hearing Vane's name, the Count inquired if he were related to the orator and statesman, George Graham Vane, whose opinions, uttered in Parliament, were still authoritative among German thinkers. This compliment to his deceased father immensely gratified, but at the same time considerably surprised, the Englishman. His father, no doubt, had been a man of much influence in the British House of Commons—a very weighty speaker, and, while in office, a first-rate administrator; but Englishmen know what a House of Commons reputation is—how fugitive, how little cosmopolitan; and that a German count should ever have heard of his father, delighted, but amazed him. In stating himself to be the son of George Graham Vane, he intimated

12*

not only the delight, but the amaze, with the frank
savoir vivre which was one of his salient characteristics.

"Sir," replied the German, speaking in very correct English, but still with his national accent, "every
German reared to political service studies England as
the school for practical thought distinct from im-
practicable theories. Long may you allow us to do so;
only excuse me one remark; never let the selfish
element of the practical supersede the generous element.
Your father never did so in his speeches, and therefore
we admired him. At the present day we don't so much
care to study English speeches. They may be insular,
—they are not European. I honour England; Heaven
grant that you may not be making sad mistakes in
the belief that you can long remain England if you
cease to be European." Herewith the German bowed,
not uncivilly—on the contrary, somewhat ceremoniously
—and disappeared with a Prussian Secretary of Embassy, whose arm he linked in his own, into a room
less frequented.

"Vicomte, who and what is your German count?"
asked Vane.

"A solemn pedant," answered the lively Vicomte—
"a German count, *que voulez-vous de plus?*"

CHAPTER VII.

A LITTLE later Graham found himself alone amongst the crowd. Attracted by the sound of music, he had strayed into one of the rooms whence it came, and in which, though his range of acquaintance at Paris was, for an Englishman, large and somewhat miscellaneous, he recognised no familiar countenance. A lady was playing the pianoforte—playing remarkably well—with accurate science, with that equal lightness and strength of finger which produces brilliancy of execution. But to appreciate her music one should be musical one's self. It wanted the charm that fascinates the un-initiated. The guests in the room were musical con-noisseurs—a class with whom Graham Vane had nothing in common. Even if he had been more capable of enjoying the excellence of the player's performance, the glance he directed towards her would have suf-ficed to chill him into indifference. She was not young, and with prominent features and puckered skin, was twisting her face into strange sentimental grimaces, as if terribly overcome by the beauty and pathos of her own melodies. To add to Vane's displeasure, she was dressed in a costume wholly antagonistic to his views of the becoming—in a Greek jacket of gold and scarlet, contrasted by a Turkish turban.

Muttering "What she-mountebank have we here!"
he sank into a chair behind the door, and fell into an
absorbed reverie. From this he was aroused by the
cessation of the music, and the hum of subdued ap-
probation by which it was followed. Above the hum
swelled the imposing voice of M. Louvier, as he rose
from a seat on the other side of the piano, by which
his bulky form had been partially concealed.

"Bravo! perfectly played—excellent! Can we not
persuade your charming young countrywoman to gratify
us even by a single song!" Then turning aside and ·
addressing some one else invisible to Graham, he said,
"Does that tyrannical doctor still compel you to silence,
Mademoiselle!"

A voice so sweetly modulated, that if there were
any sarcasm in the words it was lost in the softness
of pathos, answered, "Nay, M. Louvier, he rather over-
tasks the words at my command in thankfulness to
those who, like yourself, so kindly regard me as something else than a singer."

It was not the she-mountebank who thus spoke.
Graham rose and looked round with instinctive curiosity.
He met the face that he said had haunted him. She
too had risen, standing near the piano, with one hand
tenderly resting on the she-mountebank's scarlet and
gilded shoulder:—the face that haunted him, and yet
with a difference. There was a faint blush on the
clear pale cheek, a soft yet playful light in the grave
dark-blue eyes, which had not been visible in the
countenance of the young lady in the pearl-coloured

robe. Graham did not hear Louvier's reply, though no doubt it was loud enough for him to hear. He sank again into reverie. Other guests now came into the room, among them Frank Morley, styled Colonel —(eminent military titles in the United States do not always denote eminent military services)—a wealthy American, and his sprightly and beautiful wife. The Colonel was a clever man, rather stiff in his deportment, and grave in speech, but by no means without a vein of dry humour. By the French he was esteemed a high-bred specimen of the kind of *grand seigneur* which democratic republics engender. He spoke French like a Parisian, had an imposing presence, and spent a great deal of money with the elegance of a man of taste and the generosity of a man of heart. His high breeding was not quite so well understood by the English, because the English are apt to judge breeding by little conventional rules not observed by the American Colonel. He had a slight nasal twang, and introduced "sir" with redundant ceremony in addressing Englishmen, however intimate he might be with them, and had the habit (perhaps with a sly intention to startle or puzzle them) of adorning his style of conversation with quaint Americanisms.

Nevertheless, the genial amiability and the inherent dignity of his character made him acknowledged as a thorough gentleman by every Englishman, however conventional in tastes, who became admitted into his intimate acquaintance.

Mrs. Morley, ten or twelve years younger than

her husband, had no nasal twang, and employed no
Americanisms in her talk, which was frank, lively, and
at times eloquent. She had a great ambition to be
esteemed of a masculine understanding: Nature un-
kindly frustrated that ambition in rendering her a
model of feminine grace. Graham was intimately
acquainted with Colonel Morley; and with Mrs. Morley
had contracted one of those cordial friendships, which,
perfectly free alike from polite flirtation and Platonic
attachment, do sometimes spring up between persons
of opposite sexes without the slightest danger of changing their honest character into morbid sentimentality
or unlawful passion. The Morleys stopped to accost
Graham, but the lady had scarcely said three words
to him, before, catching sight of the haunting face,
she darted towards it. Her husband, less emotional,
bowed at the distance, and said, "To my taste, sir,
the Signorina Cicogna is the loveliest girl in the
present *bee*,* and full of mind, sir."

"Singing mind," said Graham, sarcastically, and in
the ill-natured impulse of a man striving to check his
inclination to admire.

"I have not heard her sing," replied the American,
drily; "and the words 'singing mind' are doubtless
accurately English, since you employ them; but at
Boston the collocation would be deemed barbarous.
You fly off the handle. The epithet, sir, is not in
concord with the substantive."

* *Bee*, a common expression in "the West," for a meeting or gathering
of people.

"Boston would be in the right, my dear ColoneL I stand rebuked; mind has little to do with singing."

"I take leave to deny that, sir. You fire into the wrong flock, and would not hazard the remark if you had conversed as I have with Signorina Cicogna."

Before Graham could answer, Signorina Cicogna stood before him leaning lightly on Mrs. Morley's arm.

"Frank, you must take us into the refreshment-room," said Mrs. Morley to her husband; and then, turning to Graham, added, "Will you help to make way for us?"

Graham bowed, and offered his arm to the fair speaker.

"No," said she, taking her husband's. "Of course you know the Signorina, or, as we usually call her, Mademoiselle Cicogna. No? Allow me to present you—Mr. Graham Vane—Mademoiselle Cicogna. Mademoiselle speaks English like a native."

And thus abruptly Graham was introduced to the owner of the haunting face. He had lived too much in the great world all his life to retain the innate shyness of an Englishman, but he certainly was confused and embarrassed when his eyes met Isaura's, and he felt her hand on his arm. Before quitting the room she paused and looked back — Graham's look followed her own, and saw behind them the lady with the scarlet jacket escorted by some portly and decorated connoisseur. Isaura's face brightened to another kind of brightness — a pleased and tender light.

"Poor dear *Madre*," she murmured to herself in Italian.

"*Madre*," echoed Graham, also in Italian. "I have been misinformed, then: that lady is your mother."

Isaura laughed a pretty low silvery laugh, and replied in English, "She is not my mother, but I call her *Madre*, for I know no name more loving."

Graham was touched, and said gently, "Your own mother was evidently very dear to you."

Isaura's lip quivered, and she made a slight movement as if she would have withdrawn her hand from his arm. He saw that he had offended or wounded her, and with the straightforward frankness natural to him, resumed quickly—

"My remark was impertinent in a stranger; forgive it."

"There is nothing to forgive, Monsieur."

The two now threaded their way through the crowd, both silent. At last Isaura, thinking she ought to speak first in order to show that Graham had not offended her, said—

"How lovely Mrs. Morley is!"

"Yes, and I like the spirit and ease of her American manner: have you known her long, Mademoiselle?"

"No; we met her for the first time some weeks ago at M. Savarin's."

"Was she very eloquent on the rights of women?"

"What! you have heard her on that subject?"

"I have rarely heard her on any other, though she

is the best and perhaps the cleverest friend I have at
Paris; but that may be my fault, for I like to start it.
It is a relief to the languid small-talk of society to
listen to any one thoroughly in earnest upon turning
the world topsy-turvy."

"Do you suppose poor Mrs. Morley would seek to
do that if she had her rights?" asked Isaura, with her
musical laugh.

"Not a doubt of it; but perhaps you share her
opinions."

"I scarcely know what her opinions are, but——"

"Yes—but?——"

"There is a—what shall I call it?—a persuasion—
a sentiment—out of which the opinions probably spring
that I do share."

"Indeed? a persuasion, a sentiment, for instance,
that a woman should have votes in the choice of
legislators, and, I presume, in the task of legisla-
tion?"

"No, that is not what I mean. Still, that is an
opinion, right or wrong, which grows out of the sentiment I speak of."

"Pray explain the sentiment."

"It is always so difficult to define a sentiment, but
does it not strike you that in proportion as the tendency of modern civilisation has been to raise women
more and more to an intellectual equality with men
—in proportion as they read and study and think—
an uneasy sentiment, perhaps querulous, perhaps un-
reasonable, grows up within their minds that the con-

ventions of the world are against the complete deve-
lopment of the faculties thus aroused and the ambition
thus animated;—that they cannot but rebel, though it
may be silently, against the notions of the former
age, when women were not thus educated; notions
that the aim of the sex should be to steal through
life unremarked; that it is a reproach to be talked
of; that women are plants to be kept in a hot-
house and forbidden the frank liberty of growth in
the natural air and sunshine of heaven. This, at least,
is a sentiment which has sprung up within myself, and
I imagine that it is the sentiment which has given birth
to many of the opinions or doctrines that seem absurd, and very likely are so, to the general public. I
don't pretend even to have considered those doctrines.
I don't pretend to say what may be the remedies for
the restlessness and uneasiness I feel. I doubt if on
this earth there be any remedies; all I know is, that I
feel restless and uneasy."

Graham gazed on her countenance as she spoke,
with an astonishment not unmingled with tenderness
and compassion—astonishment at the contrast between
a vein of reflection so hardy, expressed in a style of
language that seemed to him so masculine, and the
soft velvet dreamy eyes, the gentle tones, and delicate
purity of hues rendered younger still by the blush that
deepened their bloom.

At this moment they had entered the refreshment-
room; but a dense group being round the table, and
both perhaps forgetting the object for which Mrs.

Morley had introduced them to each other, they had mechanically seated themselves on an ottoman in a recess while Isaura was yet speaking. It must seem as strange to the reader as it did to Graham that such a speech should have been spoken by so young a girl to an acquaintance so new. But in truth Isaura was very little conscious of Graham's presence. She had got on a subject that perplexed and tormented her solitary thoughts—she was but thinking aloud.

"I believe," said Graham, after a pause, "that I comprehend your sentiment much better than I do Mrs. Morley's opinions; but permit me one observation. You say, truly, that the course of modern civilisation has more or less affected the relative position of woman cultivated beyond that level on which she was formerly contented to stand—the nearer perhaps to the heart of man because not lifting her head to his height;—and hence a sense of restlessness, uneasiness. But do you suppose that, in this whirl and dance of the atoms which compose the rolling ball of the civilised world, it is only women that are made restless and uneasy? Do you not see amid the masses congregated in the wealthiest cities of the world, writhings and struggles against the received order of things? In this sentiment of discontent there is a certain truthfulness, because it is an element of human nature; and how best to deal with it is a problem yet unsolved. But in the opinions and doctrines to which, among the masses, the sentiment gives birth, the wisdom of the wisest detects only the certainty of a

common ruin, offering for reconstruction the same
building materials as the former edifice—materials not
likely to be improved because they may be defaced.
Ascend from the working classes to all others in which
civilised culture prevails, and you will find that same
restless feeling—the fluttering of untried wings against
the bars between wider space and their longings.
Could you poll all the educated ambitious young men
in England—perhaps in Europe—at least half of them,
divided between a reverence for the past and a curiosity as to the future, would sigh, 'I am born a century
too late or a century too soon!'"

Isaura listened to this answer with a profound and
absorbing interest. It was the first time that a clever
young man talked thus sympathetically to her, a clever
young girl.

Then rising, he said, "I see your *Madre* and our
American friends are darting angry looks at me.
They have made room for us at the table, and are
wondering why I should keep you thus from the good
things of this little life. One word more ere we join
them—Consult your own mind, and consider whether
your uneasiness and unrest are caused solely by conventional shackles on your sex. Are they not equally
common to the youth of ours?—common to all who
seek in art, in letters, nay, in the stormier field of active life, to clasp as a reality some image yet seen but
as a dream?"

CHAPTER VIII.

No further conversation in the way of sustained dialogue took place that evening between Graham and Isaura.

The Americans and the Savarins clustered round Isaura when they quitted the refreshment-room. The party was breaking up. Vane would have offered his arm again to Isaura, but M. Savarin had forestalled him. The American was despatched by his wife to see for the carriage; and Mrs. Morley said, with her wonted sprightly tone of command—

"Now, Mr. Vane, you have no option but to take care of me to the shawl-room."

Madame Savarin and Signora Venosta had each found their cavaliers, the Italian still retaining hold of the portly connoisseur, and the Frenchwoman accepting the safeguard of the Vicomte de Brézé. As they descended the stairs, Mrs. Morley asked Graham what he thought of the young lady to whom she had presented him.

"I think she is charming," answered Graham.

"Of course; that is the stereotyped answer to all such questions, especially by you Englishmen. In public or in private, England is the mouthpiece of platitudes."

"It is natural for an American to think so. Every child that has just learned to speak uses bolder expressions than its grandmamma; but I am rather at a loss to know by what novelty of phrase an American would have answered your question."

"An American would have discovered that Isaura Cicogna had a soul, and his answer would have confessed it."

"It strikes me that he would then have uttered a platitude more stolid than mine. Every Christian knows that the dullest human being has a soul. But, to speak frankly, I grant that my answer did not do justice to the Signorina, nor to the impression she makes on me; and putting aside the charm of the face, there is a charm in a mind that seems to have gathered stores of reflection which I should scarcely have expected to find in a young lady brought up to be a professional singer."

"You add prejudice to platitude, and are horribly prosaic to-night; but here we are in the shawl-room. I must take another opportunity of attacking you. Pray dine with us to-morrow; you will meet our Minister and a few other pleasant friends."

"I suppose I must not say, 'I shall be charmed,'" answered Vane; "but I shall be."

"*Bon Dieu!* that horrid fat man has deserted Signora Venosta—looking for his own cloak, I daresay. Selfish monster!—go and hand her to her carriage—quick, it is announced!"

Graham, thus ordered, hastened to offer his arm

to the she-mountebank. Somehow she had acquired
dignity in his eyes, and he did not feel the least
ashamed of being in contact with the scarlet jacket.

The Signora grappled to him with a confiding
familiarity.

"I am afraid," she said in Italian, as they passed
along the spacious hall to the *porte cochère*—"I am
afraid that I did not make a good effect to-night—I
was nervous; did not you perceive it?"

"No, indeed; you enchanted us all," replied the
dissimulator.

"How amiable you are to say so!—you must think
that I sought for a compliment. So I did—you
gave me more than I deserved. Wine is the milk
of old men, and praise of old women. But an old
man may be killed by too much wine, and an old
woman lives all the longer for too much praise—*buona
notte.*"

Here she sprang, lithesomely enough, into the
carriage, and Isaura followed, escorted by M. Savarin.
As the two men returned towards the shawl-room, the
Frenchman said, "Madame Savarin and I complain
that you have not let us see so much of you as we
ought. No doubt you are greatly sought after;
but are you free to take your soup with us the
day after to-morrow? You will meet the Count
von Rudesheim and a few others more lively if less
wise."

"The day after to-morrow I will mark with a white

stone. To dine with M. Savarin is an event to a man who covets distinction."

"Such compliments reconcile an author to his trade. You deserve the best return I can make you. You will meet *la belle Isaure.* I have just engaged her and her *chaperon.* She is a girl of true genius, and genius is like those objects of virtu which belong to a former age, and become every day more scarce and more precious."

Here they encountered Colonel Morley and his wife hurrying to their carriage. The American stopped Vane, and whispered, "I am glad, sir, to hear from my wife that you dine with us to-morrow. Sir, you will meet Mademoiselle Cicogna, and I am not without a kinkle* that you will be enthused."

"'This seems like a fatality," soliloquised Vane as he walked through the deserted streets towards his lodging. "I strove to banish that haunting face from my mind. I had half forgotten it, and now——" Here his murmur sank into silence. He was deliberating in very conflicted thought whether or not he should write to refuse the two invitations he had accepted.

"Pooh!" he said at last, as he reached the door of his lodging, "is my reason so weak that it should be influenced by a mere superstition? Surely I know myself too well, and have tried myself too long, to fear that I should be untrue to the duty and ends of my life, even if I found my heart in danger of suffering."

* A notion.

Certainly the Fates do seem to mock our resolves to keep our feet from their ambush, and our hearts from their snare.

How our lives may be coloured by that which seems to us the most trivial accident, the merest chance! Suppose that Alain de Rochebriant had been invited to that *réunion* at M. Louvier's, and Graham Vane had accepted some other invitation and passed his evening elsewhere, Alain would probably have been presented to Isaura—what then might have happened? The impression Isaura had already made upon the young Frenchman was not so deep as that made upon Graham; but then, Alain's resolution to efface it was but commenced that day, and by no means yet confirmed. And if *he* had been the first clever young man to talk earnestly to that clever young girl, who can guess what impression he might have made upon her? His conversation might have had less philosophy and strong sense than Graham's, but more of poetic sentiment and fascinating romance.

However, the history of events that do not come to pass is not in the chronicle of the Fates.

———

usl.

BOOK III.

THE next day the guests at the Morleys' had assembled when Vane entered. His apology for unpunctuality was cut short by the lively hostess: "Your pardon is granted without the humiliation of asking for it; we know that the characteristic of the English is always to be a little behindhand."

She then proceeded to introduce him to the American Minister, to a distinguished American poet, with a countenance striking for mingled sweetness and power, and one or two other of her countrymen sojourning at Paris; and this ceremony over, dinner was announced, and she bade Graham offer his arm to Mademoiselle Cicogna.

"Have you ever visited the United States, Mademoiselle?" asked Vane, as they seated themselves at the table.

"No."

"It is a voyage you are sure to make soon."

"Why so?"

"Because report says you will create a great sensation at the very commencement of your career; and the New World is ever eager to welcome each celebrity that is achieved in the Old; more especially that which belongs to your enchanting art."

"True, sir," said an American senator, solemnly striking into the conversation; "we are an appreciative people; and if that lady be as fine a singer as I am told, she might command any amount of dollars."

Isaura coloured, and turning to Graham, asked him in a low voice if he were fond of music.

"I ought of course to say 'yes,'" answered Graham, in the same tone; "but I doubt if that 'yes' would be an honest one. In some moods, music—if a kind of music I like—affects me very deeply; in other moods, not at all. And I cannot bear much at a time. A concert wearies me shamefully; even an opera always seems to me a great deal too long. But I ought to add that I am no judge of music; that music was never admitted into my education; and, between ourselves, I doubt if there be one Englishman in five hundred who would care for opera or concert if it were not the fashion to say he did. Does my frankness revolt you?"

"On the contrary—I sometimes doubt, especially of late, if I am fond of music myself."

"Signorina—pardon me—it is impossible that you should not be. Genius can never be untrue to itself, and must love that in which it excels—that by which it communicates joy, and," he added, with a half-suppressed sigh, "attains to glory."

"Genius is a divine word, and not to be applied to a singer," said Isaura, with a humility in which there was an earnest sadness.

Graham was touched and startled; but before he could answer, the American Minister appealed to him across the table, asking if he had quoted accurately a passage in a speech by Graham's distinguished father, in regard to the share which England ought to take in the political affairs of Europe.

The conversation now became general; very political and very serious. Graham was drawn into it, and grew animated and eloquent.

Isaura listened to him with admiration. She was struck by what seemed to her a nobleness of sentiment which elevated his theme above the level of commonplace polemics. She was pleased to notice, in the attentive silence of his intelligent listeners, that they shared the effect produced on herself. In fact, Graham Vane was a born orator, and his studies had been those of a political thinker. In common talk he was but the accomplished man of the world, easy and frank and genial, with a touch of good-natured sarcasm. But when the subject started drew him upward to those heights in which politics become the science of humanity, he seemed a changed being. His cheek glowed, his eye brightened, his voice mellowed into richer tones, his language became unconsciously adorned. In such moments there might scarcely be an audience, even differing from him in opinion, which would not have acknowledged his spell.

When the party adjourned to the *salon*, Isaura said softly to Graham, "I understand why you did not cultivate music; and I think, too, that I can now under-

stand what effects the human voice can produce on
human minds, without recurring to the art of song."

"Ah," said Graham, with a pleased smile, "do not
make me ashamed of my former rudeness by the revenge of compliment, and, above all, do not disparage
your own art by supposing that any prose effect of
voice in its utterance of mind can interpret that which
music alone can express, even to listeners so uncul-
tured as myself. Am I not told truly by musical com-
posers, when I ask them to explain in words what they
say in their music, that such explanation is impossible,
that music has a language of its own untranslatable
by words?"

"Yes," said Isaura, with thoughtful brow but
brightening eyes, "you are told truly. It was only the
other day that I was pondering over that truth."

"But what recesses of mind, of heart, of soul, this
untranslatable language penetrates and brightens up!
How incomplete the grand nature of man—though
man the grandest—would be, if you struck out of his
reason the comprehension of poetry, music, and religion! In each are reached and are sounded deeps in
his reason otherwise concealed from himself. History,
knowledge, science, stop at the point in which mystery
begins. There they meet with the world of shadow.
Not an inch of that world can they penetrate without
the aid of poetry and religion, two necessities of intellectual man much more nearly allied than the votaries
of the practical and the positive suppose. To the aid
and elevation of both those necessities comes in music,

and there has never existed a religion in the world which has not demanded music as its ally. If, as I said frankly, it is only in certain moods of my mind that I enjoy music, it is only because in certain moods of my mind I am capable of quitting the guidance of prosaic reason for the world of shadow; that I am so susceptible as at every hour, were my nature perfect, I should be to the mysterious influences of poetry and religion. Do you understand what I wish to express?"

"Yes, I do, and clearly."

"Then, Signorina, you are forbidden to undervalue the gift of song. You must feel its power over the heart, when you enter the opera-house; over the soul, when you kneel in a cathedral."

"Oh," cried Isaura, with enthusiasm, a rich glow mantling over her lovely face, "how I thank you! Is it you who say you do not love music? How much better you understand it than I did till this moment!"

Here Mrs. Morley, joined by the American poet, came to the corner in which the Englishman and the singer had niched themselves. The poet began to talk, the other guests gathered round, and every one listened reverentially till the party broke up. Colonel Morley handed Isaura to her carriage—the she-mountebank again fell to the lot of Graham.

"Signor," said she, as he respectfully placed her shawl round her scarlet-and-gilt jacket, "are we so far from Paris that you cannot spare the time to call? My child does not sing in public, but at home you can hear her. It is not every woman's voice that is sweetest at home."

Graham bowed, and said he would call on the morrow.

Isaura mused in silent delight over the words which had so extolled the art of the singer. Alas, poor child! she could not guess that in those words, reconciling her to the profession of the stage, the speaker was pleading against his own heart.

There was in Graham's nature, as I think it commonly is in that of most true orators, a wonderful degree of *intellectual conscience* which impelled him to acknowledge the benignant influences of song, and to set before the young singer the noblest incentives to the profession to which he deemed her assuredly destined. But in so doing he must have felt that he was widening the gulf between her life and his own; perhaps he wished to widen it in proportion as he dreaded to listen to any voice in his heart which asked if the gulf might not be overleapt.

CHAPTER IL

On the morrow Graham called at the villa at A***. The two ladies received him in Isaura's chosen sitting-room.

Somehow or other, conversation at first languished. Graham was reserved and distant, Isaura shy and embarrassed.

The Venosta had the *frais* of making talk to her-self. Probably at another time Graham would have been amused and interested in the observation of a character new to him, and thoroughly southern— lovable, not more from its *naïve* simplicity of kind-liness than from various little foibles and vanities, all of which were harmless, and some of them endearing as those of a child whom it is easy to make happy, and whom it seems so cruel to pain: and with all the Venosta's deviations from the polished and tranquil good taste of the *beau monde*, she had that indescribable grace which rarely deserts a Florentine, so that you might call her odd but not vulgar; while, though uneducated, except in the way of her old profession, and never having troubled herself to read anything but a *libretto*, and the pious books commended to her by her confessor, the artless babble of her talk every now and then flashed out with a quaint humour, lighting up terse fragments of the old Italian wisdom which had mysteriously embedded themselves in the groundwork of her mind.

But Graham was not at this time disposed to judge the poor Venosta kindly or fairly. Isaura had taken high rank in his thoughts. He felt an impatient resentment mingled with anxiety and compassionate tenderness at a companionship which seemed to him derogatory to the position he would have assigned to a creature so gifted, and unsafe as a guide amidst the perils and trials to which the youth, the beauty, and the destined profession of Isaura were exposed. Like most Englishmen—especially Englishmen wise in the knowledge of life—he held in fastidious regard the proprieties and conventions by which the dignity of woman is fenced round; and of those proprieties and conventions the Venosta naturally appeared to him a very unsatisfactory guardian and representative.

Happily unconscious of these hostile prepossessions, the elder Signora chatted on very gaily to the visitor. She was in excellent spirits; people had been very civil to her both at Colonel Morley's and M. Louvier's. The American Minister had praised the scarlet jacket. She was convinced she had made a sensation two nights running. When the *amour propre* is pleased, the tongue is freed.

The Venosta ran on in praise of Paris and the Parisians, of Louvier and his *soirée* and the pistachio ice; of the Americans and a certain *crême de maraschino* which she hoped the Signor Inglese had not failed to taste—the *crème de maraschino* led her thoughts back to Italy. Then she grew mournful—how she missed the native *beau ciel!* Paris was pleasant, but how absurd to call it "*le Paradis des Femmes*"—as if *les Femmes* could find Paradise in a *brouillard!*

"But," she exclaimed, with vivacity of voice and gesticulation, "the Signor does not come to hear the parrot talk. He is engaged to come that he may hear the nightingale sing. A drop of honey attracts the fly more than a bottle of vinegar."

Graham could not help smiling at this adage. "I submit," said he, "to your comparison as regards myself; but certainly anything less like a bottle of vinegar than your amiable conversation I cannot well conceive. However, the metaphor apart, I scarcely know how I dare ask Mademoiselle to sing after the confession I made to her last night."

"What confession?" asked the Venosta.

"That I know nothing of music, and doubt if I can honestly say that I am fond of it."

"Not fond of music! Impossible! You slander yourself. He who loves not music would have a dull time of it in heaven. But you are English, and perhaps have only heard the music of your own country. Bad, very bad—a heretic's music! Now listen."

Seating herself at the piano, she began an air from the "*Lucia*," crying out to Isaura to come and sing to her accompaniment.

"Do you really wish it?" asked Isaura of Graham fixing on him questioning timid eyes.

"I cannot say how much I wish to hear you."

Isaura moved to the instrument, and Graham stood behind her. Perhaps he felt that he should judge more impartially of her voice if not subjected to the charm of her face.

But the first note of the voice held him spell-bound: in itself, the organ was of the rarest order, mellow and rich, but so soft that its power was lost in its sweetness, and so exquisitely fresh in every note.

But the singer's charm was less in voice than in feeling—she conveyed to the listener so much more than was said by the words, or even implied by the music. Her song in this caught the art of the painter who impresses the mind with the consciousness of a something which the eye cannot detect on the canvas.

She seemed to breathe out from the depths of her heart the intense pathos of the original romance, so far exceeding that of the opera—the human tenderness, the mystic terror of a tragic love-tale more solemn in its sweetness than that of Verona.

When her voice died away no applause came—not even a murmur. Isaura bashfully turned round to steal a glance at her silent listener, and beheld moistened eyes and quivering lips. At that moment she was reconciled to her art. Graham rose abruptly and walked to the window.

"Do you doubt now if you are fond of music?" cried the Venosta.

"This is more than music," answered Graham, still with averted face. Then, after a short pause, he

approached Isaura and said, with a melancholy half-
smile—

"I do not think, Mademoiselle, that I could dare
to hear you often; it would take me too far from the
hard real world; and he who would not be left behindhand on the road that he must journey cannot indulge
frequent excursions into fairy-land."

"Yet," said Isaura, in a tone yet sadder, "I was
told in my childhood, by one whose genius gives
authority to her words, that beside the real world lies
the ideal. The real world then seemed rough to me.
'Escape,' said my counsellor, 'is granted from that
stony thoroughfare into the fields beyond its formal
hedgerows. The ideal world has its sorrows, but it
never admits despair.' That counsel then, methought,
decided my choice of life. I know not now if it has
done so."

"Fate," answered Graham, slowly and thoughtfully
— "Fate, which is not the ruler but the servant of
Providence, decides our choice of life, and rarely from
outward circumstances. Usually the motive power is
within. We apply the word genius to the minds of
the gifted few; but in all of us there is a genius that
is inborn, a pervading something which distinguishes
our very identity, and dictates to the conscience that
which we are best fitted to do and to be. In so dic-
tating it compels our choice of life; or if we resist the
dictate, we find at the close that we have gone astray.
My choice of life thus compelled is on the stony
thoroughfares—yours in the green fields."

As he thus said, his face became clouded and mournful.

The Venosta, quickly tired of a conversation in which she had no part, and having various little household matters to attend to, had during this dialogue slipped unobserved from the room; yet neither Isaura nor Graham felt the sudden consciousness that they were alone which belongs to lovers.

"Why," asked Isaura, with that magic smile reflected in countless dimples which, even when her words were those of a man's reasoning, made them seem gentle with a woman's sentiment— "why must your road through the world be so exclusively the stony one? It is not from necessity—it cannot be from taste. And whatever definition you give to genius, surely it is not your own inborn genius that dictates to you a constant exclusive adherence to the commonplace of life."

"Ah, Mademoiselle! do not misrepresent me. I did not say that I could not sometimes quit the real world for fairy-land—I said that I could not do so often. My vocation is not that of a poet or artist."

"It is that of an orator, I know," said Isaura, kindling;— "so they tell me, and I believe them. But is not the orator somewhat akin to the poet? Is not oratory an art?"

"Let us dismiss the word orator: as applied to English public life, it is a very deceptive expression. The Englishman who wishes to influence his countrymen by force of words spoken must mix with them in their beaten thoroughfares—must make himself master of their practical views and interests—must be conversant with their prosaic occupations and business —must understand how to adjust their loftiest aspirations to their material welfare—must avoid, as the fault most dangerous to himself and to others, that kind of eloquence which is called oratory in France, and which has helped to make the French the worst politicians in Europe. Alas, Mademoiselle! I fear that an English statesman would appear to you a very dull orator."

"I see that I spoke foolishly—yes, you show me that the world of the statesman lies apart from that of the artist. Yet——"

"Yet what?"

"May not the ambition of both be the same?"

"How so?"

"To refine the rude, to exalt the mean—to identify their own fame with some new beauty, some new glory, added to the treasure-house of all."

Graham bowed his head reverently, and then raised it with the flush of enthusiasm on his cheek and brow.

"Oh, Mademoiselle!" he exclaimed, "what a sure guide and what a noble inspirer to a true Englishman's ambition nature has fitted you to be, were it not——" He paused abruptly.

This outburst took Isaura utterly by surprise. She had been accustomed to the language of compliment till it had begun to pall, but a compliment of this

14 *

kind was the first that had ever reached her ear.
She had no words in answer to it; involuntarily she
placed her hand on her heart as if to still its beatings.
But the unfinished exclamation, "Were it not,"
troubled her more than the preceding words had flattered—and mechanically she murmured, "Were it not
—what?"

"Oh," answered Graham, affecting a tone of gaiety,
"I felt too ashamed of my selfishness as man to finish
my sentence."

"Do so, or I shall fancy you refrained lest you
might wound me as woman."

"Not so—on the contrary; had I gone on it would
have been to say that a woman of your genius, and
more especially of such mastery in the most popular
and fascinating of all arts, could not be contented if
she inspired nobler thoughts in a single breast—she
must belong to the public, or rather the public must
belong to her: it is but a corner of her heart that an
individual can occupy, and even that individual must
merge his existence in hers—must be contented to
reflect a ray of the light she sheds on admiring
thousands. Who could dare to say to you, 'Renounce
your career—confine your genius, your art, to the petty
circle of home'? To an actress—a singer—with whose
fame the world rings, home would be a prison. Pardon
me, pardon——"

Isaura had turned away her face to hide tears that
would force their way, but she held out her hand to
him with a childlike frankness, and said softly, "I am

not offended." Graham did not trust himself to continue the same strain of conversation. Breaking into a new subject, he said, after a constrained pause, "Will you think it very impertinent in so new an acquaintance, if I ask how it is that you, an Italian, know our language as a native? and is it by Italian teachers that you have been trained to think and to feel?"

"Mr. Selby, my second father, was an Englishman, and did not speak any other language with comfort to himself. He was very fond of me—and had he been really my father I could not have loved him more: we were constant companions till—till I lost him."

"And no mother left to console you." Isaura shook her head mournfully, and the Venosta here re-entered.

Graham felt conscious that he had already stayed too long, and took leave.

They knew that they were to meet that evening at the Savarins'.

To Graham that thought was not one of unmixed pleasure; the more he knew of Isaura, the more he felt self-reproach that he had allowed himself to know her at all.

But after he had left, Isaura sang low to herself the song which had so affected her listener; then she fell into abstracted reverie, but she felt a strange and new sort of happiness. In dressing for M. Savarin's dinner, and twining the classic ivy wreath into her dark locks, her Italian servant exclaimed, "How beautiful the Signorina looks to-night!"

CHAPTER IIL

M. SAVARIN was one of the most brilliant of that galaxy of literary men which shed lustre on the reign of Louis Philippe.

His was an intellect peculiarly French in its lightness and grace. Neither England nor Germany nor America has produced any resemblance to it. Ireland has, in Thomas Moore; but then in Irish genius there is so much that is French.

M. Savarin was free from the ostentatious extravagance which had come into vogue with the Empire. His house and establishment were modestly maintained within the limit of an income chiefly, perhaps entirely, derived from literary profits.

Though he gave frequent dinners, it was but to few at a time, and without show or pretence. Yet the dinners, though simple, were perfect of their kind; and the host so contrived to infuse his own playful gaiety into the temper of his guests, that the feasts at his house were considered the pleasantest at Paris. On this occasion the party extended to ten, the largest number his table admitted.

All the French guests belonged to the Liberal party, though in changing tints of the tricolor. *Place aux dames*, first to be named were the Countess de

Craon and Madame Vertot—both without husbands.
The Countess had buried the Count, Madame Vertot
had separated from Monsieur. The Countess was very
handsome, but she was sixty. Madame Vertot was
twenty years younger, but she was very plain. She
had quarrelled with the distinguished author for whose
sake she had separated from Monsieur, and no man
had since presumed to think that he could console
a lady so plain for the loss of an author so distinguished.

Both these ladies were very clever. The Countess
had written lyrical poems entitled 'Cries of Liberty,'
and a drama of which Danton was the hero, and the
moral too revolutionary for admission to the stage;
but at heart the Countess was not at all a revolution-
ist—the last person in the world to do or desire anything that could bring a washerwoman an inch nearer
to a countess. She was one of those persons who play
with fire in order to appear enlightened.

Madame Vertot was of severer mould. She had
knelt at the feet of M. Thiers, and went into the
historico-political line. She had written a remarkable
book upon the modern Carthage (meaning England),
and more recently a work that had excited much attention upon the Balance of Power, in which she proved
it to be the interest of civilisation and the necessity
of Europe that Belgium should be added to France,
and Prussia circumscribed to the bounds of its original
margraviate. She showed how easily these two objects
could have been effected by a constitutional monarch

instead of an egotistical Emperor. Madame Vertot was
a decided Orleanist.

Both these ladies condescended to put aside author-
ship in general society. Next amongst our guests let
me place the Count de Passy and *Madame son épouse:*
the Count was seventy-one, and, it is needless to add,
a type of Frenchman rapidly vanishing, and not likely
to find itself renewed. How shall I describe him so
as to make my English reader understand? Let me
try by analogy. Suppose a man of great birth and
fortune, who in his youth had been an enthusiastic
friend of Lord Byron and a jocund companion of
George IV.—who had in him an immense degree of
lofty romantic sentiment with an equal degree of well-
bred worldly cynicism, but who, on account of that
admixture, which is rare, kept a high rank in either of
the two societies into which, speaking broadly, civilised
life divides itself—the romantic and the cynical. The
Count de Passy had been the most ardent among the
young disciples of Châteaubriand—the most brilliant
among the young courtiers of Charles X. Need I add
that he had been a terrible lady-killer?

But in spite of his admiration of Châteaubriand
and his allegiance to Charles X., the Count had been
always true to those caprices of the French *noblesse*
from which he descended—caprices which destroyed
them in the old Revolution—caprices belonging to the
splendid ignorance of their nation in general and their
order in particular. Speaking without regard to partial
exceptions, the French *gentilhomme* is essentially a Pa-

risian; a Parisian is essentially impressionable to the impulse or fashion of the moment. Is it *à la mode* for the moment to be Liberal or anti-Liberal? Parisians embrace and kiss each other, and swear through life and death to adhere for ever to the *mode* of the moment. The Three Days were the *mode* of the moment—the Count de Passy became an enthusiastic Orleanist. Louis Philippe was very gracious to him. He was decorated—he was named *préfet* of his department—he was created senator—he was about to be sent Minister to a German Court when Louis Philippe fell. The Republic was proclaimed. The Count caught the popular contagion, and after exchanging tears and kisses with patriots whom a week before he had called *canaille*, he swore eternal fidelity to the Republic. The fashion of the moment suddenly became Napoleonic, and with the *coup d'état* the Republic was metamorphosed into an Empire. The Count wept on the bosoms of all the *Vieilles Moustaches* he could find, and rejoiced that the sun of Austerlitz had rearisen. But after the affair of Mexico the sun of Austerlitz waxed very sickly. Imperialism was fast going out of fashion. The Count transferred his affection to Jules Favre, and joined the ranks of the advanced Liberals. During all these political changes, the Count had remained very much the same man in private life; agreeable, good-natured, witty, and, above all, a devotee of the fair sex. When he had reached the age of sixty-eight he was still *fort bel homme*—unmarried, with a grand presence and charming manner. At that

age he said, "*Je me range*," and married a young lady
of eighteen. She adored her husband, and was wildly
jealous of him; while the Count did not seem at all
jealous of her, and submitted to her adoration with a
gentle shrug of the shoulders.

The three other guests who, with Graham and the
two Italian ladies, made up the complement of ten,
were the German Count von Rudesheim, a celebrated
French physician named Bacourt, and a young author
whom Savarin had admitted into his clique and declared to be of rare promise. This author, whose real
name was Gustave Rameau, but who, to prove, I suppose, the sincerity of that scorn for ancestry which he
professed, published his verses under the patrician designation of Alphonse de Valcour, was about twenty-
four, and might have passed at the first glance for
younger; but, looking at him closely, the signs of old
age were already stamped on his visage.

He was undersized, and of a feeble slender frame.
In the eyes of women and artists the defects of his
frame were redeemed by the extraordinary beauty of
the face. His black hair, carefully parted in the centre,
and worn long and flowing, contrasted the whiteness
of a high though narrow forehead, and the delicate
pallor of his cheeks. His features were very regular,
his eyes singularly bright; but the expression of the
face spoke of fatigue and exhaustion—the silky locks
were already thin, and interspersed with threads of
silver—the bright eyes shone out from sunken orbits

—the lines round the mouth were marked as they are in the middle age of one who has lived too fast.

It was a countenance that might have excited a compassionate and tender interest, but for something arrogant and supercilious in the expression—something that demanded not tender pity but enthusiastic admiration. Yet that expression was displeasing rather to men than to women; and one could well conceive that, among the latter, the enthusiastic admiration it challenged would be largely conceded.

The conversation at dinner was in complete contrast to that at the American's the day before. There the talk, though animated, had been chiefly earnest and serious—here it was all touch and go, sally and repartee. The subjects were the light *on dits* and lively anecdotes of the day, not free from literature and politics, but both treated as matters of *persiflage*, hovered round with a jest and quitted with an epigram. The two French lady authors, the Count de Passy, the physician, and the host, far outshone all the other guests. Now and then, however, the German Count struck in with an ironical remark condensing a great deal of grave wisdom, and the young author with ruder and more biting sarcasm. If the sarcasm told, he showed his triumph by a low-pitched laugh; if it failed, he evinced his displeasure by a contemptuous sneer or a grim scowl.

Isaura and Graham were not seated near each other, and were for the most part contented to be listeners.

On adjourning to the *salon* after dinner, Graham, however, was approaching the chair in which Isaura had placed herself, when the young author, forestalling him, dropped into the seat next to her, and began a conversation in a voice so low that it might have passed for a whisper. The Englishman drew back and observed them. He soon perceived, with a pang of jealousy not unmingled with scorn, that the author's talk appeared to interest Isaura. She listened with evident attention; and when she spoke in return, though Graham did not hear her words, he could observe on her expressive countenance an increased gentleness of aspect.

"I hope," said the physician, joining Graham, as most of the other guests gathered round Savarin, who was in his liveliest vein of anecdote and wit—"I hope that the fair Italian will not allow that ink-bottle imp to persuade her that she has fallen in love with him."

"Do young ladies generally find him so seductive!" asked Graham, with a forced smile.

"Probably enough. He has the reputation of being very clever and very wicked, and that is a sort of character which has the serpent's fascination for the daughters of Eve."

"Is the reputation merited?"

"As to the cleverness, I am not a fair judge. I dislike that sort of writing which is neither manlike nor womanlike, and in which young Rameau excels. He has the knack of finding very exaggerated phrases by which to express common-place thoughts. He writes

verses about love in words so stormy that you might
fancy that Jove was descending upon Semele. But
when you examine his words, as a sober pathologist
like myself is disposed to do, your fear for the peace
of households vanishes—they are ' *Vox et præterea
nihil*'—no man really in love would use them. He
writes prose about the wrongs of humanity. You feel
for humanity. You say, 'Grant the wrongs, now for
the remedy,' and you find nothing but balderdash.
Still I am bound to say that both in verse and prose
Gustave Rameau is in unison with a corrupt taste of
the day, and therefore he is coming into vogue. So
much as to his writings: as to his wickedness, you
have only to look at him to feel sure that he is not a
hundredth part so wicked as he wishes to seem. In a
word, then, Mons. Gustave Rameau is a type of that
somewhat numerous class among the youth of Paris,
which I call 'the lost Tribe of Absinthe.' There is a
set of men who begin to live full gallop while they
are still boys. As a general rule, they are originally
of the sickly frames which can scarcely even trot, much
less gallop, without the spur of stimulants, and no
stimulant so fascinates their peculiar nervous system
as absinthe. The number of patients in this set who
at the age of thirty are more worn out than septuagena-
rians, increases so rapidly as to make one dread to
think what will be the next race of Frenchmen. To
the predilection for absinthe young Rameau and the
writers of his set add the imitation of Heine, after, indeed, the manner of caricaturists, who effect a likeness

striking in proportion as it is ugly. It is not easy to
imitate the pathos and the wit of Heine; but it is easy
to imitate his defiance of the Deity, his mockery of
right and wrong, his relentless war on that heroic
standard of thought and action which the writers who
exalt their nation intuitively preserve. Rameau cannot
be a Heine, but he can be to Heine what a misshapen
snarling dwarf is to a mangled blaspheming Titan. Yet
he interests the women in general, and he evidently
interests the fair Signorina in especial."

Just as Bacourt finished that last sentence, Isaura
lifted the head which had hitherto bent in an earnest
listening attitude that seemed to justify the Doctor's
remarks, and looked round. Her eyes met Graham's
with the fearless candour which made half the charm
of their bright yet soft intelligence. But she dropped
them suddenly with a half-start and a change of colour,
for the expression of Graham's face was unlike that
which she had hitherto seen on it—it was hard, stern,
somewhat disdainful. A minute or so afterwards she
rose, and in passing across the room towards the group
round the host, paused at a table covered with books
and prints near to which Graham was standing—alone.
The Doctor had departed in company with the German
Count.

Isaura took up one of the prints.

"Ah!" she exclaimed, "Sorrento—my Sorrento.
Have you ever visited Sorrento, Mr. Vane?"

Her question and her movement were evidently
in conciliation. Was the conciliation prompted by

coquetry, or by a sentiment more innocent and artless?

Graham doubted, and replied coldly, as he bent
over the print—

"I once stayed there a few days, but my recol-
lection of it is not sufficiently lively to enable me to
recognise its features in this design."

"That is the house, at least so they say, of Tasso's
father; of course you visited that?"

"Yes, it was a hotel in my time; I lodged there."

"And I too. There I first read 'the Gerusalemme.'"
The last words were said in Italian, with a low mea-
sured tone, inwardly and dreamily.

A somewhat sharp and incisive voice speaking in
French here struck in and prevented Graham's re-
joinder: "*Quel joli dessin!* What is it, Mademoiselle?"

Graham recoiled: the speaker was Gustave Rameau,
who had, unobserved, first watched Isaura, then rejoined her side.

"A view of Sorrento, Monsieur, but it does not
do justice to the place. I was pointing out the house
which belonged to Tasso's father."

"Tasso! *Hein!* and which is the fair Eleonora's?"

"Monsieur," answered Isaura, rather startled at
that question from a professed *homme de lettres*, "Eleonora did not live at Sorrento."

"*Tant pis pour Sorrente,*" said the *homme de lettres*,
carelessly. "No one would care for Tasso if it were
not for Eleonora."

"I should rather have thought," said Graham, "that

no one would have cared for Eleonora if it were not
for Tasso."

Rameau glanced at the Englishman superciliously.

"*Pardon*, Monsieur—in every age a love-story
keeps its interest; but who cares nowadays for *le clinquant du Tasse?*"

"*Le clinquant du Tasse!*" exclaimed Isaura, indignantly.

"The expression is Boileau's, Mademoiselle, in ridicule of the '*Sot de qualité*,' who prefers

'*Le clinquant du Tasse à tout l'or de Virgile.*'

But for my part I have as little faith in the last as
the first."

"I do not know Latin, and have therefore not read
Virgil," said Isaura.

"Possibly," remarked Graham, "Monsieur does not
know Italian, and has therefore not read Tasso."

"If that be meant in sarcasm," retorted Rameau,
"I construe it as a compliment. A Frenchman who
is contented to study the masterpieces of modern
literature need learn no language and read no authors
but his own."

Isaura laughed her pleasant silvery laugh. "I
should admire the frankness of that boast, Monsieur,
if in our talk just now you had not spoken as con-
temptuously of what we are accustomed to consider
French masterpieces as you have done of Virgil and
Tasso."

"Ah, Mademoiselle! it is not my fault if you have

had teachers of taste so *rococo* as to bid you find masterpieces in the tiresome stilted tragedies of Corneille and Racine. Poetry of a court, not of a people —one simple novel, one simple stanza that probes the hidden recesses of the human heart, reveals the sores of this wretched social state, denounces the evils of superstition, kingcraft, and priestcraft, is worth a library of the rubbish which pedagogues call 'the classics.' We agree, at least, in one thing, Mademoiselle; we both do homage to the genius of your friend Madame de Grantmesnil."

"Your friend, Signorina!" cried Graham, incredulously; "is Madame de Grantmesnil your friend?"

"The dearest I have in the world."

Graham's face darkened; he turned away in silence, and in another minute vanished from the room, persuading himself that he felt not one pang of jealousy in leaving Gustave Rameau by the side of Isaura. "Her dearest friend Madame de Grantmesnil!"—he muttered.

A word now on Isaura's chief correspondent. Madame de Grantmesnil was a woman of noble birth and ample fortune. She had separated from her husband in the second year after marriage. She was a singularly eloquent writer, surpassed among contemporaries of her sex in popularity and renown only by Georges Sand.

At least as fearless as that great novelist in the frank exposition of her views, she had commenced her career in letters by a work of astonishing power

and pathos, directed against the institution of marriage
as regulated in Roman Catholic communities. I do
not know that it said more on this delicate subject
than the English Milton has said; but then Milton did
not write for a Roman Catholic community, nor adopt
a style likely to captivate the working classes. Madame de Grantmesnil's first book was deemed an attack on the religion of the country, and captivated
those among the working classes who had already ab-
jured that religion. This work was followed up by
others more or less in defiance of 'received opinions;'
some with political, some with social revolutionary
aim and tendency, but always with a singular purity
of style. Search all her books, and however you might
revolt from her doctrine, you could not find a hazard-
ous expression. The novels of English young ladies
are naughty in comparison. Of late years, whatever
might be hard or audacious in her political or social
doctrines, softened itself into charm amid the golden
haze of romance. Her writings had grown more and
more purely artistic—poetising what is good and
beautiful in the realities of life, rather than creating a
false ideal out of what is vicious and deformed.
Such a woman, separated young from her husband,
could not enunciate such opinions and lead a life so
independent and uncontrolled as Madame de Grantmesnil had done, without scandal, without calumny.
Nothing, however, in her actual life, had ever been so
proved against her as to lower the high position she
occupied in right of birth, fortune, renown. Wher-

ever she went she was *fêlée*—as in England foreign
princes, and in America foreign authors, are *fêlés*.
Those who knew her well concurred in praise of her
lofty, generous, lovable qualities.   Madame de Grantmesnil had known Mr. Selby; and when, at his death,
Isaura, in the innocent age between childhood and
youth, had been left the most sorrowful and most
lonely creature on the face of the earth, this famous
woman, worshipped by the rich for her intellect, adored
by the poor for her beneficence, came to the orphan's
friendless side, breathing love once more into her
pining heart, and waking for the first time the desires
of genius, the aspirations of art, in the dim self-con-
sciousness of a soul between sleep and waking.

But, my dear Englishman, put yourself in Graham's
place, and suppose that you were beginning to fall in
love with a girl whom for many good reasons you
ought not to marry; suppose that in the same hour in
which you were angrily conscious of jealousy on account of a man whom it wounds your self-esteem to
consider a rival, the girl tells you that her dearest
friend is a woman who is famed for her hostility to
the institution of marriage!

CHAPTER IV.

On the same day in which Graham dined with the Savarins, M. Louvier assembled round his table the *élite* of the young Parisians who constituted the oligarchy of fashion, to meet whom he had invited his new friend the Marquis de Rochebriant. Most of them belonged to the Legitimist party—the *noblesse* of the *faubourg;* those who did not, belonged to no political party at all,—indifferent to the cares of mortal states as the gods of Epicurus. Foremost among this *Jeunesse dorée* were Alain's kinsmen, Raoul and Enguerrand de Vandemar. To these Louvier introduced him with a burly parental *bonhomie,* as if he were the head of the family. "I need not bid you, young folks, to make friends with each other. A Vandemar and a Rochebriant are not made friends—they are born friends." So saying he turned to his other guests.

Almost in an instant Alain felt his constraint melt away in the cordial warmth with which his cousins greeted him.

These young men had a striking family likeness to each other, and yet in feature, colouring, and expression, in all save that strange family likeness, they were contrasts.

Raoul was tall, and, though inclined to be slender,

with sufficient breadth of shoulder to indicate no inconsiderable strength of frame. His hair worn short, and his silky beard worn long, were dark, so were his eyes, shaded by curved drooping lashes; his complexion was pale, but clear and healthful. In repose the expression of his face was that of a somewhat melancholy indolence, but in speaking it became singularly sweet, with a smile of the exquisite urbanity which no artificial politeness can bestow; it must emanate from that native high breeding which has its source in goodness of heart.

Enguerrand was fair, with curly locks of a golden chestnut. He wore no beard, only a small moustache rather darker than his hair. His complexion might in itself be called effeminate, its bloom was so fresh and delicate, but there was so much of boldness and energy in the play of his countenance, the hardy outline of the lips, and the open breadth of the forehead, that "effeminate" was an epithet no one ever assigned to his aspect. He was somewhat under the middle height, but beautifully proportioned, carried himself well, and somehow or other did not look short even by the side of tall men. Altogether he seemed formed to be a mother's darling, and spoiled by women, yet to hold his own among men with a strength of will more evident in his look and his bearing than it was in those of his graver and statelier brother.

Both were considered by their young co-equals models in dress, but in Raoul there was no sign that care or thought upon dress had been bestowed; the simplicity of his costume was absolute and severe. On his plain shirt-front there gleamed not a stud, on his fingers there sparkled not a ring. Enguerrand, on the contrary, was not without pretension in his attire; the *broderie* in his shirt-front seemed woven by the Queen of the Fairies. His rings of turquoise and opal, his studs and wrist-buttons of pearl and brilliants, must have cost double the rental of Rochebriant, but probably they cost him nothing. He was one of those happy Lotharios to whom Calistas make constant presents. All about him was so bright that the atmosphere around seemed gayer for his presence.

In one respect at least the brothers closely resembled each other—in that exquisite graciousness of manner for which the genuine French noble is traditionally renowned—a graciousness that did not desert them even when they came reluctantly into contact with *roturiers* or republicans; but the graciousness became *égalité, fraternité* towards one of their caste and kindred.

"We must do our best to make Paris pleasant to you," said Raoul, still retaining in his grasp the hand he had taken.

"*Vilain cousin,*" said the livelier Enguerrand, "to have been in Paris twenty-four hours, and without letting us know."

"Has not your father told you that I called upon him?"

"Our father," answered Raoul, "was not so savage as to conceal that fact, but he said you were only here on business for a day or two, had declined his invitation, and would not give your address. *Pauvre père!* we scolded him well for letting you escape from us thus. My mother has not forgiven him yet; we must present you to her to-morrow. I answer for your liking her almost as much as she will like you."

Before Alain could answer dinner was announced. Alain's place at dinner was between his cousins. How pleasant they made themselves! it was the first time in which Alain had been brought into such familiar conversation with countrymen of his own rank as well as his own age. His heart warmed to them. The general talk of the other guests was strange to his ear; it ran much upon horses and races, upon the opera and the ballet; it was enlivened with satirical anecdotes of persons whose names were unknown to the Provincial—not a word was said that showed the smallest interest in politics or the slightest acquaintance with literature. The world of these well-born guests seemed one from which all that concerned the great mass of mankind was excluded, yet the talk was that which could only be found in a very polished society; in it there was not much wit, but there was a prevalent vein of gaiety, and the gaiety was never violent, the laughter was never loud; the scandals circulated might imply cynicism the most absolute, but in language the most refined. The Jockey Club of Paris has its perfume.

Raoul did not mix in the general conversation; he devoted himself pointedly to the amusement of his cousin, explaining to him the point of the anecdotes circulated, or hitting off in terse sentences the characters of the talkers.

Enguerrand was evidently of temper more vivacious than his brother, and contributed freely to the current play of light gossip and mirthful sally.

Louvier, seated between a duke and a Russian prince, said little, except to recommend a wine or an *entrée*, but kept his eye constantly on the Vandemars and Alain.

Immediately after coffee the guests departed. Before they did so, however, Raoul introduced his cousin to those of the party most distinguished by hereditary rank or social position. With these the name of Rochebriant was too historically famous not to insure respect of its owner; they welcomed him among them as if he were their brother.

The French duke claimed him as a connection by an alliance in the fourteenth century; the Russian prince had known the late Marquis, and 'trusted that the son would allow him to improve into friendship the acquaintance he had formed with the father.'

Those ceremonials over, Raoul linked his arm in Alain's, and said: "I am not going to release you so soon after we have caught you. You must come with me to a house in which I at least spend an hour or two every evening. I am at home there. Bah! I take no refusal. Do not suppose I carry you off to Bohemia, a country which, I am sorry to say, Enguerrand now and then visits, but which is to me as unknown as the mountains of the moon. The house I speak of is *comme il faut* to the utmost. It is that of the Contessa di Rimini—a charming Italian by marriage, but by birth and in character *on ne peut plus Française.* My mother adores her."

That dinner at M. Louvier's had already effected a great change in the mood and temper of Alain de Rochebriant; he felt, as if by magic, the sense of youth, of rank, of station, which had been so suddenly checked and stifled, warmed to life within his veins. He should have deemed himself a boor had he refused the invitation so frankly tendered.

But on reaching the *coupé* which the brothers kept in common, and seeing it only held two, he drew back.

"Nay, enter, *mon cher*," said Raoul, divining the cause of his hesitation; "Enguerrand has gone on to his club."

CHAPTER V.

"TELL me," said Raoul, when they were in the carriage, "how you came to know M. Louvier."

"He is my chief mortgagee."

"H'm! that explains it. But you might be in worse hands; the man has a character for liberality."

"Did your father mention to you my circumstances, and the reason that brings me to Paris?"

"Since you put the question point-blank, my dear cousin, he did."

"He told you how poor I am, and how keen must be my life-long struggle to keep Rochebriant as the home of my race."

"He told us all that could make us still more respect the Marquis de Rochebriant, and still more eagerly long to know our cousin and the head of our house," answered Raoul, with a certain nobleness of tone and manner.

Alain pressed his kinsman's hand with grateful emotion.

"Yet," he said, falteringly, "your father agreed with me that my circumstances would not allow me to——"

"Bah!" interrupted Raoul with a gentle laugh; "my father is a very clever man, doubtless, but he knows only the world of his own day, nothing of the world of ours. I and Enguerrand will call on you to-morrow, to take you to my mother, and before doing so, to consult as to affairs in general. On this last matter Enguerrand is an oracle. Here we are at the Contessa's."

CHAPTER VI.

THE Contessa di Rimini received her visitors in a
boudoir furnished with much apparent simplicity, but
a simplicity by no means inexpensive. The draperies
were but of chintz, and the walls covered with the
same material, a lively pattern, in which the prevalents
were rose-colour and white; but the ornaments on the
mantelpiece, the china stored in the cabinets or arranged on the shelves, the small nick-nacks scattered
on the tables, were costly rarities of art.

The Contessa herself was a woman who had somewhat passed her thirtieth year, not strikingly handsome, but exquisitely pretty. "There is," said a great
French writer, "only one way in which a woman can
be handsome, but a hundred thousand ways in which
she can be pretty;" and it would be impossible to
reckon up the number of ways in which Adeline di
Rimini carried off the prize in prettiness.

Yet it would be unjust to the personal attractions
of the Contessa to class them all under the word
'prettiness.' When regarded more attentively, there
was an expression in her countenance that might almost be called divine, it spoke so unmistakably of a
sweet nature and an untroubled soul. An English
poet once described her by repeating the old lines,—

"Her face is like the milky way i' the sky,—
A meeting of gentle lights without a name."

She was not alone; an elderly lady sate on an
arm-chair by the fire, engaged in knitting; and a man,
also elderly, and whose dress proclaimed him an ec-
clesiastic, sate at the opposite corner, with a large
Angora cat on his lap.

"I present to you, Madame," said Raoul, "my new-
found cousin, the seventeenth Marquis de Rochebriant,
whom I am proud to consider, on the male side, the
head of our house, representing its eldest branch:
welcome him for my sake—in future he will be welcome for his own."

The Contessa replied very graciously to this introduction, and made room for Alain on the divan from
which she had risen.

The old lady looked up from her knitting, the ec-
clesiastic removed the cat from his lap. Said the old
lady, "I announce myself to M. le Marquis; I knew
his mother well enough to be invited to his christen-
ing; otherwise I have no pretension to the acquaintance
of a cavalier *si beau*,—being old—rather deaf—very
stupid—exceedingly poor——"

"And," interrupted Raoul, "the woman in all Paris,
the most adored for *bonté*, and consulted for *savoir
vivre* by the young cavaliers whom she deigns to receive. Alain, I present you to Madame de Maury, the
widow of a distinguished author and academician, and
the daughter of the brave Henri de Gerval, who fought
for the good cause in La Vendée. I present you also

to the Abbé Vertpré, who has passed his life in the
vain endeavour to make other men as good as himself."

"Base flatterer!" said the Abbé, pinching Raoul's
ear with one hand, while he extended the other to
Alain. "Do not let your cousin frighten you from
knowing me, M. le Marquis; when he was my pupil,
he so convinced me of the incorrigibility of perverse
human nature, that I now chiefly address myself to
the moral improvement of the brute creation. Ask
the Contessa if I have not achieved a *beau succès* with
her Angora cat. Three months ago that creature had
the two worst propensities of man. He was at once
savage and mean; he bit, he stole. Does he ever bite
now? No. Does he ever steal? No. Why? I have
awakened in that cat the dormant conscience, and that
done, the conscience regulates his actions: once made
aware of the difference between wrong and right, the
cat maintains it unswervingly, as if it were a law of
nature. But if, with prodigious labour, one does awaken
conscience in a human sinner, it has no steady effect
on his conduct—he continues to sin all the same.
Mankind at Paris, Monsieur le Marquis, is divided between two classes—one bites and the other steals:
shun both; devote yourself to cats."

The Abbé delivered this oration with a gravity of
mien and tone which made it difficult to guess whether
he spoke in sport or in earnest—in simple playfulness
or with latent sarcasm.

But on the brow and in the eye of the priest there

was a general expression of quiet benevolence, which made Alain incline to the belief that he was only speaking as a pleasant humorist; and the Marquis replied gaily—

"Monsieur l'Abbé, admitting the superior virtue of cats, when taught by so intelligent a preceptor, still the business of human life is not transacted by cats; and since men must deal with men, permit me, as a preliminary caution, to inquire in which class I must rank yourself. Do you bite or do you steal?"

This sally, which showed that the Marquis was already shaking off his provincial reserve, met with great success.

Raoul and the Contessa laughed merrily; Madame de Maury clapped her hands, and cried *"Bien!"*

The Abbé replied, with unmoved gravity, "Both. I am a priest; it is my duty to bite the bad and steal from the good, as you will see, M. le Marquis, if you will glance at this paper."

Here he handed to Alain a memorial on behalf of an afflicted family who had been burnt out of their home, and reduced from comparative ease to absolute want. There was a list appended of some twenty subscribers, the last being the Contessa, fifty francs, and Madame de Maury, five.

"Allow me, Marquis," said the Abbé, "to steal from you; bless you twofold, *mon fils!*" (taking the napoleon Alain extended to him)—"first for your charity—secondly, for the effect of its example upon the heart of your cousin. Raoul de Vandemar, stand and deliver. Bah!—what! only ten francs."

Raoul made a sign to the Abbé, unperceived by the rest, as he answered, "Abbé, I should excel your expectations of my career if I always continue worth half as much as my cousin."

Alain felt to the bottom of his heart the delicate tact of his richer kinsman in giving less than himself, and the Abbé replied, "Niggard, you are pardoned. Humility is a more difficult virtue to produce than charity, and in your case an instance of it is so rare that it merits encouragement."

The 'tea equipage' was now served in what at Paris is called the English fashion; the Contessa presided over it, the guests gathered round the table, and the evening passed away in the innocent gaiety of a domestic circle. The talk, if not especially intellectual, was at least not fashionable—books were not discussed, neither were scandals; yet somehow or other it was cheery and animated, like that of a happy family in a country-house. Alain thought still the better of Raoul that, Parisian though he was, he could appreciate the charm of an evening so innocently spent.

On taking leave, the Contessa gave Alain a general invitation to drop in whenever he was not better engaged.

"I except only the opera nights," said she. "My husband has gone to Milan on his affairs, and during his absence I do not go to parties; the opera I cannot resist."

Raoul set Alain down at his lodgings. "*Au revoir;* to-morrow at one o'clock expect Enguerrand and myself."

CHAPTER VII.

RAOUL and Enguerrand called on Alain at the hour fixed.

"In the first place," said Raoul, "I must beg you to accept my mother's regrets that she cannot receive you to-day. She and the Contessa belong to a society of ladies formed for visiting the poor, and this is their day; but to-morrow you must dine with us *en famille*. Now to business. Allow me to light my cigar while you confide the whole state of affairs to Enguerrand: whatever he counsels, I am sure to approve."

Alain, as briefly as he could, stated his circumstances, his mortgages, and the hopes which his *avoué* had encouraged him to place in the friendly disposition of M. Louvier. When he had concluded, Enguerrand mused for a few moments before replying. At last he said, "Will you trust me to call on Louvier on your behalf? I shall but inquire if he is inclined to take on himself the other mortgages; and if so, on what terms. Our relationship gives me the excuse for my interference; and to say truth, I have had much familiar intercourse with the man. I too am a speculator, and have often profited by Louvier's advice. You may ask what can be his object in serving me; he can gain nothing by it. To this I answer, the key

to his good offices is in his character. Audacious
though he be as a speculator, he is wonderfully prudent as a politician. This *belle France* of ours is like
a stage tumbler; one can never be sure whether it will
stand on its head· or its feet. Louvier very wisely
wishes to feel himself safe whatever party comes up-
permost. He has no faith in the duration of the Empire; and as, at all events, the Empire will not con-
fiscate his millions, he takes no trouble in conciliating
Imperialists. But on the principle which induces certain savages to worship the devil and neglect the *bon
Dieu*, because the devil is spiteful and the *bon Dieu* is
too beneficent to injure them, Louvier, at heart detest-
ing as well as dreading a republic, lays himself out to
secure friends with the Republicans of all classes, and
pretends to espouse their cause. Next to them, he is
very conciliatory to the Orleanists. Lastly, though he
thinks the Legitimists have no chance, he desires to
keep well with the nobles of that party, because they
exercise a considerable influence over that sphere of
opinion which belongs to fashion; for fashion is never
powerless in Paris. Raoul and myself are no mean
authorities in *salons* and clubs; and a good word from
us is worth having.

"Besides, Louvier himself in his youth set up for a
dandy; and that deposed ruler of dandies, our un-
fortunate kinsman, Victor de Mauléon, shed some of
his own radiance on the money-lender's son. But
when Victor's star was eclipsed, Louvier ceased to
gleam. The dandies cut him. In his heart he exults

that the dandies now throng to his *soirées*. *Bref*, the *millionnaire* is especially civil to me—the more so as I know intimately two or three eminent journalists; and Louvier takes pains to plant garrisons in the press. I trust I have explained the grounds on which I may be a better diplomatist to employ than your *avoué;* and with your leave I will go to Louvier at once."

"Let him go," said Raoul. "Enguerrand never fails in anything he undertakes, especially," he added, with a smile half sad, half tender, "when one wishes to replenish one's purse."

"I too gratefully grant such an ambassador all powers to treat," said Alain. "I am only ashamed to consign to him a post so much beneath his genius," and 'his birth' he was about to add, but wisely checked himself. Enguerrand said, shrugging his shoulders, "You can't do me a greater kindness than by setting my wits at work. I fall a martyr to *ennui* when I am not in action," he said, and was gone.

"It makes me very melancholy at times," said Raoul, flinging away the end of his cigar, "to think that a man so clever and so energetic as Enguerrand should be as much excluded from the service of his country as if he were an Iroquois Indian. He would have made a great diplomatist."

"Alas!" replied Alain, with a sigh, "I begin to doubt whether we Legitimists are justified in maintaining a useless loyalty to a sovereign who renders us morally exiles in the land of our birth."

"I have no doubt on the subject," said Raoul.

16 *

"We are not justified on the score of policy, but we have no option at present on the score of honour. We should gain so much for ourselves if we adopted the State livery and took the State wages that no man would esteem us as patriots; we should only be de-·spised as apostates. So long as Henry V. lives, and does not resign his claim, we cannot be active citizens; we must be mournful lookers-on. But what matters it? We nobles of the old race are becoming rapidly extinct. Under any form of government likely to be established in France we are equally doomed. The French people, aiming at an impossible equality, will never again tolerate a race of *gentilshommes*. They cannot prevent, without destroying commerce and capital altogether, a quick succession of men of the day, who form nominal aristocracies much more op-posed to equality than any hereditary class of nobles. But they refuse these fleeting substitutes of born pa-tricians all permanent stake in the country, since whatever estate they buy must be subdivided at their death. My poor Alain, you are making it the one ambition of your life to preserve to your posterity the home and lands of your forefathers. How is that possible, even supposing you could redeem the mort-gages? You marry some day—you have children, and Rochebriant must then be sold to pay for their sepa-rate portions. How this condition of things, while rendering us so ineffective to perform the normal functions of a *noblesse* in public life, affects us in pri-.vate life, may be easily conceived.

"Condemned to a career of pleasure and frivolity, we can scarcely escape from the contagion of extravagant luxury which forms the vice of the time. With grand names to keep up, and small fortunes whereon to keep them, we readily incur embarrassment and debt. Then neediness conquers pride. We cannot be great merchants, but we can be small gamblers on the Bourse, or, thanks to the *Crédit Mobilier*, imitate a cabinet minister, and keep a shop under another name. Perhaps you have heard that Enguerrand and I keep a shop. Pray, buy your gloves there. Strange fate for men whose ancestors fought in the first Crusade —*mais que voulez vous?*"

"I was told of the shop," said Alain, "but the moment I knew you I disbelieved the story."

"Quite true. Shall I confide to you why we resorted to that means of finding ourselves in pocket-money? My father gives us rooms in his hotel; the use of his table, which we do not much profit by; and an allowance, on which we could not live as young men of our class live at Paris. Enguerrand had his means of spending pocket-money, I mine; but it came to the same thing—the pockets were emptied. We incurred debts. Two years ago my father straitened himself to pay them, saying, 'The next time you come to me with debts, however small, you must pay them yourselves, or you must marry, and leave it to me to find you wives.' This threat appalled us both. A month afterwards, Enguerrand made a lucky hit at the Bourse, and proposed to invest the proceeds in a shop. I resisted as long as I could, but Enguerrand triumphed over me, as he always does. He found an excellent deputy in a *bonne* who had nursed us in childhood, and married a journeyman perfumer who understands the business. It answers well; we are not in debt, and we have preserved our freedom."

After these confessions Raoul went away, and Alain fell into a mournful reverie, from which he was roused by a loud ring at his bell. He opened the door, and beheld M. Louvier. The burly financier was much out of breath after making so steep an ascent. It was in gasps that he muttered, "*Bonjour;* excuse me if I derange you." Then entering and seating himself on a chair, he took some minutes to recover speech, rolling his eyes staringly round the meagre, unluxurious room, and then concentrating their gaze upon its occupier.

"*Peste,* my dear Marquis!" he said at last, "I hope the next time I visit you the ascent may be less arduous. One would think you were in training to ascend the Himalaya."

The haughty noble writhed under this jest, and the spirit inborn in his order spoke in his answer.

"I am accustomed to dwell on heights, M. Louvier; the castle of Rochebriant is not on a level with the town."

An angry gleam shot from the eyes of the *millionnaire*, but there was no other sign of displeasure in his answer.

"*Bien dit, mon cher:* how you remind me of your father! Now, give me leave to speak on affairs. I have seen your cousin Enguerrand de Vandemar. *Homme de moyens* though *joli garçon.* He proposed that you should call on me. I said 'no' to the *cher petit* Enguerrand—a visit from me was due to you. To cut matters short, M. Gandrin has allowed me to look into your papers. I was disposed to serve you from the first—I am still more disposed to serve you now. I undertake to pay off all your other mortgages, and become sole mortgagee, and on terms that I have jotted down on this paper, and which I hope will content you."

He placed a paper in Alain's hand, and took out a box, from which he extracted a jujube, placed it in his mouth, folded his hands, and reclined back in his chair, with his eyes half closed, as if exhausted alike by his ascent and his generosity.

In effect, the terms were unexpectedly liberal. The reduced interest on the mortgages would leave the Marquis an income of £1000 a-year instead of £400. Louvier proposed to take on himself the legal cost of transfer, and to pay to the Marquis 25,000 francs, on the completion of the deed, as a bonus. The mortgage did not exempt the building-land, as Hébert desired. In all else it was singularly advantageous, and Alain could but feel a thrill of grateful delight at an offer by which his stinted income was raised to comparative affluence.

"Well, Marquis," said Louvier, "what does the castle say to the town 1"

"M. Louvier," answered Alain, extending his hand with cordial eagerness, "accept my sincere apologies for the indiscretion of my metaphor. Poverty is proverbially sensitive to jests on it. I owe it to you if I cannot hereafter make that excuse for any words of mine that may displease you. The terms you propose are most liberal, and I close with them at once."

"*Bon*," said Louvier, shaking vehemently the hand offered to him; "I will take the paper to Gandrin, and instruct him accordingly. And now, may I attach a condition to the agreement which is not put down on paper? It may have surprised you perhaps that I should propose a gratuity of 25,000 francs on completion of the contract. It is a droll thing to do, and not in the ordinary way of business, therefore I must explain. Marquis, pardon the liberty I take, but you have inspired me with an interest in your future. With your birth, connections, and figure, you should push your way in the world far and fast. But you can't do so in a province. You must find your opening at Paris. I wish you to spend a year in the capital, and live, not extravagantly, like a *nouveau riche*, but in a way not unsuited to your rank, and permitting you all the social advantages that belong to it. These 25,000 francs, in addition to your improved income, will enable you to gratify my wish in this respect. Spend the money in Paris: you will want every *sou* of it in the course of the year. It will be money well spent. Take my advice, *cher Marquis. Au plaisir.*"

The financier bowed himself out. The young Marquis forgot all the mournful reflections with which Raoul's conversation had inspired him. He gave a new touch to his toilet, and sallied forth with the air of a man on whose morning of life a sun heretofore clouded has burst forth and bathed the landscape in its light.

CHAPTER VIII.

SINCE the evening spent at the Savarins', Graham
had seen no more of Isaura. He had avoided all
chance of seeing her—in fact, the jealousy with which
he had viewed her manner towards Rameau, and the
angry amaze with which he had heard her proclaim
her friendship for Madame de Grantmesnil, served to
strengthen the grave and secret reasons which made
him desire to keep his heart yet free and his hand
yet unpledged. But, alas! the heart was enslaved already. It was under the most fatal of all spells—first
love conceived at first sight. He was wretched; and
in his wretchedness his resolves became involuntarily
weakened. He found himself making excuses for the
beloved. What cause had he, after all, for that jealousy of the young poet which had so offended him!
and if, in her youth and inexperience, Isaura had
made her dearest friend of a great writer by whose
genius she might be dazzled, and of whose opinions
she might scarcely be aware, was it a crime that ne-
cessitated her eternal banishment from the reverence
which belongs to all manly love! Certainly he found
no satisfactory answers to such self-questionings. And
then those grave reasons known only to himself, and
never to be confided to another—why he should yet

reserve his hand unpledged—were not so imperative as to admit of no compromise. They might entail a sacrifice, and not a small one to a man of Graham's views and ambition. But what is love if it can think any sacrifice, short of duty and honour, too great to offer up unknown, uncomprehended, to the one beloved! Still, while thus softened in his feelings towards Isaura, he became, perhaps in consequence of such softening, more and more restlessly impatient to fulfil the object for which he had come to Paris, the great step towards which was the discovery of the undiscoverable Louise Duval.

He had written more than once to M. Renard since the interview with that functionary already recorded, demanding whether Renard had not made some progress in the research on which he was employed, and had received short unsatisfactory replies preaching patience and implying hope.

The plain truth, however, was, that M. Renard had taken no further pains in the matter. He considered it utter waste of time and thought to attempt a discovery to which the traces were so faint and so obsolete. If the discovery were effected, it must be by one of those chances which occur without labour or forethought of our own. He trusted only to such a chance in continuing the charge he had undertaken. But during the last day or two Graham had become yet more impatient than before, and peremptorily requested another visit from this dilatory confidant.

In that visit, finding himself pressed hard, and

though naturally willing, if possible to retain a
client, unusually generous, yet being, on the whole,
an honest member of his profession, and feeling it
to be somewhat unfair to accept large remuneration
for doing nothing, M. Renard said frankly, "Monsieur, this affair is beyond me; the keenest agent of
our police could make nothing of it. Unless you
can tell me more than you have done, I am utterly
without a clue. I resign, therefore, the task with
which you honoured me, willing to resume it again if
you can give me information that could render me of
use."

"What sort of information?"

"At least the names of some of the lady's relations
who may yet be living."

"But it strikes me that, if I could get at that piece
of knowledge, I should not require the services of the
police. The relations would tell me what had become
of Louise Duval quite as readily as they would tell a
police agent."

"Quite true, Monsieur. It would really be picking
your pockets if I did not at once retire from your
service. Nay, Monsieur, pardon me, no further pay-
ments; I have already accepted too much. Your most
obedient servant."

Graham, left alone, fell into a very gloomy reverie.
He could not but be sensible of the difficulties in the
way of the object which had brought him to Paris,
with somewhat sanguine expectations of success
founded on a belief in the omniscience of the Parisian

police, which is only to be justified when they have
to deal with a murderess or a political incendiary.
But the name of Louise Duval is about as common
in France as that of Mary Smith in England; and the
English reader may judge what would be the likely
result of inquiring through the ablest of our detectives
after some Mary Smith of whom you could give little
more information than that she was the daughter of
a drawing-master who had·died twenty years ago,
that it was about fifteen years since anything had
been heard of her, that you could not say if, through
marriage or for other causes, she had changed her
name or not, and you had reasons for declining resort to public advertisements. In the course of inquiry so instituted, the probability would be that you
might hear of a great many Mary Smiths, in the pursuit of whom your *employé* would lose all sight and
scent of the one Mary Smith for whom the chase was
instituted.

In the midst of Graham's despairing reflections his
laquais announced M. Frederic Lemercier.

"*Cher* Grarm-Varn. A thousand pardons if I disturb you at this late hour of the evening; but you remember the request you made me when you first
arrived in Paris this season?"

"Of course I do—in case you should ever chance
in your wide round of acquaintance to fall in with a
Madame or Mademoiselle Duval of about the age of
forty, or a year or so less, to let me know: and you
did fall in with two ladies of that name, but they

were not the right one—not the person whom my friend begged me to discover—both much too young."

"*Eh bien, mon cher.* If you will come with me to the *bal champêtre* in the Champs Elysées to-night, I can show you a third Madame Duval; her Christian name is Louise, too, of the age you mention—though she does her best to look younger, and is still very handsome. You said your Duval was handsome. It was only last evening that I met this lady at a *soirée* given by Mademoiselle Julie Caumartin, *coryphée distinguée,* in love with young Rameau."

"In love with young Rameau! I am very glad to hear it. He returns the love?"

"I suppose so. He seems very proud of it. But *à propos* of Madame Duval, she has been long absent from Paris—just returned—and looking out for conquests. She says she has a great *penchant* for the English; promises me to be at this ball—come."

"Hearty thanks, my dear Lemercier. I am at your service."

CHAPTER IX.

THE *bal champêtre* was gay and brilliant, as such festal scenes are at Paris. A lovely night in the midst of May—lamps below and stars above: the society mixed, of course. Evidently, when Graham has singled out Frederic Lemercier from all his acquaintances at Paris, to conjoin with the official aid of M. Renard in search of the mysterious lady, he had conjectured the probability that she might be found in the Bohemian world so familiar to Frederic; if not as an inhabitant, at least as an explorer. Bohemia was largely represented at the *bal champêtre*, but not without a fair sprinkling of what we call the 'respectable classes,' especially English and Americans, who brought their wives there to take care of them. Frenchmen, not needing such care, prudently left their wives at home. Among the Frenchmen of station were the Comte de Passy and the Vicomte de Brézé.

On first entering the gardens, Graham's eye was attracted and dazzled by a brilliant form. It was standing under a festoon of flowers extended from tree to tree, and a gas jet opposite shone full upon the face—the face of a girl in all the freshness of youth. If the freshness owed anything to art, the art was so well disguised that it seemed nature. The beauty of the countenance was Hebe-like, joyous, and radiant, and yet one could not look at the girl without a sentiment of deep mournfulness. She was surrounded by a group of young men, and the ring of her laugh jarred upon Graham's ear. He pressed Frederic's arm, and directing his attention to the girl, asked who she was.

"Who! Don't you know! That is Julie Caumartin. A little while ago her equipage was the most admired in the Bois, and great ladies condescended to copy her dress or her *coiffure*. But she has lost her splendour, and dismissed the rich admirer who supplied the fuel for its blaze, since she fell in love with Gustave Rameau. Doubtless she is expecting him to-night. You ought to know her; shall I present you?"

"No," answered Graham, with a compassionate expression in his manly face. "So young; seemingly so gay. How I pity her!"

"What! for throwing herself away on Rameau! True. There is a great deal of good in that girl's nature, if she had been properly trained. Rameau wrote a pretty poem on her which turned her head and won her heart, in which she is styled the 'Ondine of Paris,'—a nymph-like type of Paris itself."

"Vanishing type, like her namesake; born of the spray, and vanishing soon into the deep," said Graham. "Pray go and look for the Duval; you will find me seated yonder."

Graham passed into a retired alley, and threw

himself on a solitary bench, while Lemercier went in search of Madame Duval. In a few minutes the Frenchman reappeared. By his side was a lady well dressed, and as she passed under the lamps Graham perceived that, though of a certain age, she was undeniably handsome. His heart beat more quickly. Surely this was the Louise Duval he sought.

He rose from his seat, and was presented in due form to the lady, with whom Frederic then discreetly left him.

"Monsieur Lemercier tells me that you think that we were once acquainted with each other."

"Nay, Madame; I should not fail to recognise you were that the case. A friend of mine had the honour of knowing a lady of your name; and should I be fortunate enough to meet that lady, I am charged with a commission that may not be unwelcome to her. M. Lemercier tells me your *nom de baptême* is Louise."

"Louise Corinne, Monsieur."

"And I presume that Duval is the name you take from your parents."

"No; my father's name was Bernard. I married, when I was a mere child, M. Duval, in the wine trade at Bordeaux."

"Ah, indeed!" said Graham, much disappointed, but looking at her with a keen, searching eye, which she met with a decided frankness. Evidently, in his judgment, she was speaking the truth.

"You know English, I think, Madame," he resumed, addressing her in that language.

"A leetle—speak *un peu.*"

"Only a little?"

Madame Duval looked puzzled, and replied in French, with a laugh, "Is it that you were told that I spoke English by your countryman, Milord Sare Boulby? *Petit scélérat,* I hope he is well. He sends you a commission for me—so he ought: he behaved to me like a monster."

"Alas! I know nothing of Milord Sir Boulby. Were you never in England yourself?"

"Never"—with a coquettish side-glance—"I should like so much to go. I have a foible for the English in spite of that *vilain petit* Boulby. Who is it gave you the commission for me? Ha! I guess—le Capitaine Nelton."

"No. What year, Madame, if not impertinent, were you at Aix-la-Chapelle?"

"You mean Baden? I was there seven years ago, when I met le Capitaine Nelton—*bel homme aux cheveux rouges.*"

"But you have been at Aix?"

"Never."

"I have, then, been mistaken, Madame, and have only to offer my most humble apologies."

"But perhaps you will favour me with a visit, and we may on further conversation find that you are not mistaken. I can't stay now, for I am engaged to dance with the Belgian of whom, no doubt, M. Lemercier has told you."

"No, Madame, he has not."

"Well, then, he will tell you. The Belgian is very jealous. But I am always at home between three and four; this is my card."

Graham eagerly took the card, and exclaimed, "Is this your own handwriting, Madame?"

"Yes, indeed."

"*Très belle écriture*," said Graham, and receded with a ceremonious bow. "Anything so unlike *her* handwriting. Another disappointment," muttered the Englishman as the lady went back to the ball.

A few minutes later Graham joined Lemercier, who was talking with De Passy and De Brézé.

"Well," said Lemercier, when his eye rested on Graham, "I hit the right nail on the head this time, eh?"

Graham shook his head.

"What! Is she not the right Louise Duval?"

"Certainly not."

The Count de Passy overheard the name, and turned. "Louise Duval," he said; "does Monsieur Vane know a Louise Duval?"

"No; but a friend asked me to inquire after a lady of that name whom he had met many years ago at Paris." The Count mused a moment, and said, "Is it possible that your friend knew the family De Mauléon?"

"I really can't say. What then?"

"The old Vicomte de Mauléon was one of my most intimate associates. In fact, our houses are connected. And he was extremely grieved, poor man,

17*

when his daughter Louise married her drawing-master, Auguste Duval."

"Her drawing-master, Auguste Duval? Pray say on. I think the Louise Duval my friend knew must have been her daughter. She was the only child of a drawing-master or artist named Auguste Duval, and probably enough her Christian name would have been derived from her mother. A Mademoiselle de Mauléon, then, married M. Auguste Duval?"

"Yes; the old Vicomte had espoused *en premières noces* Mademoiselle Camille de Chavigny, a lady of birth equal to his own,—had by her one daughter, Louise. I recollect her well,—a plain girl, with a high nose and a sour expression. She was just of age when the first Vicomtesse died, and by the marriage settlement she succeeded at once to her mother's fortune, which was not large. The Vicomte was, however, so poor that the loss of that income was no trifle to him. Though much past fifty, he was still very handsome. Men of that generation did not age soon, Monsieur," said the Count, expanding his fine chest and laughing exultingly.

"He married, *en secondes noces*, a lady of still higher birth than the first, and with a much larger *dot*. Louise was indignant at this, hated her stepmother; and when a son was born by the second marriage she left the paternal roof, went to reside with an old female relative near the Luxembourg, and there married this drawing-master. Her father and the family did all they could to prevent it; but in these democratic days a woman who has attained her majority can, if she persist in her determination, marry to please herself and disgrace her ancestors. After that *mésalliance* her father never would see her again. I tried in vain to soften him. All his parental affections settled on his handsome Victor. Ah! you are too young to have known Victor de Mauléon during his short reign at Paris—as *roi des viveurs*."

"Yes, he was before my time; but I have heard of him as a young man of great fashion—said to be very clever, a duellist, and a sort of Don Juan."

"Exactly."

"And then I remember vaguely to have heard that he committed, or was said to have committed, some villanous action connected with a great lady's jewels, and to have left Paris in consequence."

Ah, yes—a sad scrape. At that time there was a political crisis; we were under a Republic; anything against a noble was believed. But I am sure Victor de Mauléon was not the man to commit a larceny. However, it is quite true that he left Paris, and I don't know what has become of him since." Here he touched De Brézé, who, though still near, had not been listening to this conversation, but interchanging jest and laughter with Lemercier on the motley scene of the dance.

"De Brézé, have you ever heard what became of poor dear Victor de Mauléon?—you knew him."

"Knew him! I should think so. Who could be in the great world and not know *le beau* Victor? No;

after he vanished I never heard more of him,—
doubtless long since dead. A good-hearted fellow in
spite of all his sins."

"My dear M. de Brézé, did you know his half-
sister?" asked Graham—"a Madame Duval?"

"No; I never heard he had a half-sister. Halt
there: I recollect that I met Victor once, in the garden
at Versailles, walking arm-in-arm with the most beautiful girl I ever saw; and when I complimented him
afterwards at the Jockey Club on his new conquest,
he replied very gravely that the young lady was his
niece. 'Niece!' said I; 'why, there can't be more than
five or six years between you.' 'About that, I suppose,' said he; 'my half-sister, her mother, was more
than twenty years older than I at the time of my
birth.' I doubted the truth of his story at the time;
but since you say he really had a sister, my doubt
wronged him."

"Have you never seen that same young lady
since?"

"Never."

"How many years ago was this?"

"Let me see—about twenty or twenty-one years
ago. How time flies!"

Graham still continued to question, but could
learn no farther particulars. He turned to quit the
gardens just as the band was striking up for a fresh
dance, a wild German waltz air, and mingled with
that German music his ear caught the sprightly sounds
of the French laugh, one laugh distinguished from the

rest by a more genuine ring of light-hearted joy—the laugh that he had heard on entering the gardens, and the sound of which had then saddened him. Looking toward the quarter from which it came, he again saw the 'Ondine of Paris.' She was not now the centre of a group. She had just found Gustave Rameau; and was clinging to his arm with a look of happiness in her face, frank and innocent as a child's. And so they passed amid the dancers down a solitary lamplit alley, till lost to the Englishman's lingering gaze.

CHAPTER X.

THE next morning Graham sent again for M. Renard.

· "Well," he cried, when that dignitary appeared and took a seat beside him; "chance has favoured me."

"I always counted on chance, Monsieur. Chance has more wit in its little finger than the Paris police in its whole body."

"I have ascertained the relations, on the mother's side, of Louise Duval, and the only question is how to get at them."

Here Graham related what he had heard, and ended by saying, "This Victor de Mauléon is therefore my Louise Duval's uncle. He was, no doubt, taking charge of her in the year that the persons interested in her discovery lost sight of her in Paris; and surely he must know what became of her afterwards."

"Very probably; and chance may befriend us yet in the discovery of Victor de Mauléon. You seem not to know the particulars of that story about the jewels which brought him into some connection with the police, and resulted in his disappearance from Paris."

"No; tell me the particulars."

"Victor de Mauléon was heir to some 60,000 or 70,000 francs a-year, chiefly on the mother's side; for his father, though the representative of one of the most ancient houses in Normandy, was very poor, having little of his own except the emoluments of an appointment in the Court of Louis Philippe.

"But before, by the death of his parents, Victor came into that inheritance, he very largely forestalled it. His tastes were magnificent. He took to 'sport' —kept a famous stud, was a great favourite with the English, and spoke their language fluently. Indeed he was considered very accomplished, and of considerable intellectual powers. It was generally said that some day or other, when he had sown his wild oats, he would, if he took to politics, be an eminent man. Altogether he was a very strong creature. That was a very strong age under Louis Philippe. The *viveurs* of Paris were fine types for the heroes of Dumas and Sue—full of animal life and spirits. Victor de Mauléon was a romance of Dumas—incarnated."

"M. Renard, forgive me that I did not before do justice to your taste in polite literature."

"Monsieur, a man in my profession does not attain even to my humble eminence if he be not something else than a professional. He must study mankind wherever they are described—even in *les romans*. To return to Victor de Mauléon. Though he was a 'sportman,' a gambler, a Don Juan, a duellist, nothing was ever said against his honour. On the contrary, on

matters of honour he was a received oracle; and even
though he had fought several duels (that was the age
of duels), and was reported without a superior, almost
without an equal, in either weapon—the sword or the
pistol—he is said never to have wantonly provoked
an encounter, and to have so used his skill that he
contrived never to slay, nor even gravely to wound,
an antagonist.

"I remember one instance of his generosity in this
respect, for it was much talked of at the time. One
of your countrymen, who had never handled a fencing-
foil nor fired a pistol, took offence at something M.
de Mauléon had said in disparagement of the Duke of
Wellington, and called him out. Victor de Mauléon
accepted the challenge, discharged his pistol, not in
the air—that might have been an affront—but so as
to be wide of the mark, walked up to the lines to be
shot at, and when missed, said, 'Excuse the suscepti-
bility of a Frenchman, loath to believe that his countrymen can be beaten save by accident, and accept
every apology one gentleman can make to another
for having forgotten the respect due to one of the
most renowned of your national heroes.' The Englishman's name was Vane. Could it have been your
father?"

"Very probably; just like my father to call out any
man who insulted the honour of his country, as represented by its men. I hope the two combatants became friends?"

"That I never heard; the duel was over—there my story ends."

"Pray go on."

"One day—it was in the midst of political events which would have silenced most subjects of private gossip—the *beau monde* was startled by the news that the Vicomte (he was then, by his father's death, Vicomte) de Mauléon had been given into the custody of the police on the charge of stealing the jewels of the Duchesse de—— (the wife of a distinguished foreigner). It seems that some days before this event, the Duc, wishing to make Madame his spouse an agreeable surprise, had resolved to have a diamond necklace belonging to her, and which was of setting so old-fashioned that she had not lately worn it, reset for her birthday. He therefore secretly possessed himself of the key to an iron safe in a cabinet adjoining her dressing-room (in which safe her more valuable jewels were kept), and took from it the necklace. Imagine his dismay when the jeweller in the Rue Vivienne to whom he carried it, recognised the pretended diamonds as imitation paste which he himself had some days previously inserted into an empty setting brought to him by a Monsieur with whose name he was unacquainted. The Duchesse was at that time in delicate health; and as the Duc's suspicions naturally fell on the servants, especially on the *femme de chambre*, who was in great favour with his wife, he did not like to alarm Madame, nor through her to put the servants on their guard. He resolved, therefore, to

place the matter in the hands of the famous * * *,
who was then the pride and ornament of the Parisian
police. And the very night afterwards the Vicomte
de Mauléon was caught and apprehended in the
cabinet where the jewels were kept, and to which he
had got access by a false key, or at least a duplicate
key, found in his possession. I should observe that
M. de Mauléon occupied the *entresol* in the same hotel
in which the upper rooms were devoted to the Duc
and Duchesse and their suite. As soon as this charge
against the Vicomte was made known (and it was
known the next morning), the extent of his debts and
the utterness of his ruin (before scarcely conjectured
or wholly unheeded) became public through the
medium of the journals, and furnished an obvious
motive for the crime of which he was accused. We
Parisians, Monsieur, are subject to the most startling
reactions of feeling. The men we adore one day we
execrate the next. The Vicomte passed at once from
the popular admiration one bestows on a hero, to the
popular contempt with which one regards a petty
larcener. Society wondered how it had ever condescended to receive into its bosom the gambler, the
duellist, the Don Juan. However, one compensation
in the way of amusement he might still afford to
society for the grave injuries he had done it. Society
would attend his trial, witness his demeanour at the
bar, and watch the expression of his face when he was
sentenced to the galleys. But, Monsieur, this wretch
completed the measure of his iniquities. He was not

tried at all. The Duc and Duchesse quitted Paris for Spain, and the Duc instructed his lawyer to withdraw his charge, stating his conviction of the Vicomte's complete innocence of any other offence than that which he himself had confessed."

"What did the Vicomte confess? you omitted to state that."

"The Vicomte, when apprehended, confessed that, smitten by an insane passion for the Duchesse, which she had, on his presuming to declare it, met with indignant scorn, he had taken advantage of his lodgment in the same house to admit himself into the cabinet adjoining her dressing-room by means of a key which he had procured, made from an impression of the key-hole taken in wax.

"No evidence in support of any other charge against the Vicomte was forthcoming—nothing, in short, beyond the *infraction du domicile* caused by the madness of youthful love, and for which there was no prosecution. The law, therefore, could have little to say against him. But society was more rigid; and, exceedingly angry to find that a man who had been so conspicuous for luxury should prove to be a pauper, insisted on believing that M. de Mauléon was guilty of the meaner, though not perhaps, in the eyes of husbands and fathers, the more heinous, of the two offences. I presume that the Vicomte felt that he had got into a dilemma from which no pistol-shot or sword-thrust could free him, for he left Paris abruptly, and has not since reappeared. The sale of his stud and effects sufficed, I believe, to pay his debts, for I will do him the justice to say that they were paid."

"But though the Vicomte de Mauléon has disappeared, he must have left relations at Paris, who would perhaps know what has become of him and of his niece."

"I doubt it. He had no very near relations. The nearest was an old *célibataire* of the same name, from whom he had some expectations, but who died shortly after this *esclandre*, and did not name the Vicomte in his will. M. Victor had numerous connections among the highest families—the Rochebriants, Chavignys, Vandemars, Passys, Beauvilliers. But they are not likely to have retained any connection with a ruined *vaurien*, and still less with a niece of his who was the child of a drawing-master. But now you have given me a clue, I will try to follow it up. We must find the Vicomte, and I am not without hope of doing so. Pardon me if I decline to say more at present. I would not raise false expectations. But in a week or two I will have the honour to call again upon Monsieur."

"Wait one instant. You have really a hope of discovering M. de Mauléon?"

"Yes. I cannot say more at present."

M. Renard departed.

Still that hope, however faint it might prove, served

to reanimate Graham; and with that hope his heart, as if a load had been lifted from its mainspring, returned instinctively to the thought of Isaura. Whatever seemed to promise an early discharge of the commission connected with the discovery of Louise Duval seemed to bring Isaura nearer to him, or at least to excuse his yearning desire to see more of her —to understand her better. Faded into thin air was the vague jealousy of Gustave Rameau which he had so unreasonably conceived; he felt as if it were impossible that the man whom the 'Ondine of Paris' claimed as her lover could dare to woo or hope to win an Isaura. He even forgot the friendship with the eloquent denouncer of the marriage-bond, which a little while ago had seemed to him an unpardonable offence: he remembered only the lovely face, so innocent, yet so intelligent; only the sweet voice which had for the first time breathed music into his own soul; only the gentle hand whose touch had for the first time sent through his veins the thrill which distinguishes from all her sex the woman whom we love. He went forth elated and joyous, and took his way to Isaura's villa. As he went, the leaves on the trees under which he passed seemed stirred by the soft May breeze in sympathy with his own delight. Perhaps it was rather the reverse: his own silent delight sympathised with all delight in awakening nature. The lover seeking reconciliation with the loved one from whom some trifle has unreasonably estranged him, in a cloudless day of May,—if he be not happy enough to feel a brotherhood in all things happy—a leaf in bloom; a bird in song—then indeed he may call himself lover, but he does not know what is love.

END OF VOL. L

PRINTING OFFICE OF THE PUBLISHER.